She was gone.

Like a figment of his i_____ _____ remnant
of a dream. Justin knew she had been real. The
ache of his body and the lingering scent of her, of
them, of sex, lingered on his skin and on the tangle
of sheets bunched around his waist.

He eased out of bed, grabbing his discarded
pants and then slipping them on as he navigated
the detritus of their amazing night together flung
all over the space of the penthouse suite: empty
glasses and bottles on the floor alongside the
remnants of an early-morning room service order of
celebratory steak and lobster.

And...her wedding veil.

It was one of those cheap ones sold by every
wedding chapel on the strip. When she'd slipped it
on, the combination of sex-on-wheels and virginal
sacrifice had decimated what had been left of his
very iffy mind, and he'd marched down the aisle and
said two words he'd never planned on saying in his
life: *I do*.

He'd gone to Vegas for a poker game and married a
complete stranger.

A stranger who had left in the middle of the night.

* * *

Seducing His Secret Wife by Robin Covington is
part of the Redhawk Reunion series.

Dear Reader,

The Redhawk Reunion series continues with the exciting romance of Sarina Redhawk and Justin Ling!

I love a prickly, complicated heroine. Sarina Redhawk has a difficult past, a complicated present and an uncertain future. But she's used to things not coming easily for her, and her relationship with Justin Ling is anything but easy. It's hot, forbidden and a secret that has the potential to derail the next big deal for his company, Redhawk/Ling.

And it's quite possibly the best thing that will ever happen to her.

Of course, she doesn't know it and she'll fight it every step of the way. And that is what made it so much fun to write. Pairing the serious, wounded Sarina with the push-the-envelope, take-all-the-chances Justin was an indulgence of my love of opposites-attract romance. And writing a secret Vegas wedding?

So. Much. Fun.

And this book continues the reunion of the Redhawk siblings. Two Cherokee brothers and a sister separated when they were children were just recently brought back together and are trying to figure out how to be a family again and reconnect with their culture and their community.

So, this book contains everything I love about Harlequin Desire romance: passion, glamour, emotional high stakes and family.

If you adore Sarina and Justin as much as I do, let me know on social media! I'd love to hear from you.

Xoxo,

Robin

ROBIN COVINGTON

———

SEDUCING HIS SECRET WIFE

HARLEQUIN
DESIRE

HARLEQUIN®
DESIRE™

Recycling programs for this product may not exist in your area.

ISBN-13: 978-1-335-23274-8

Seducing His Secret Wife

Copyright © 2021 by Robin Ray Coll

This edition published by arrangement with Harlequin Books S.A.

For questions and comments about the quality of this book, please contact us at CustomerService@Harlequin.com.

Harlequin Enterprises ULC
22 Adelaide St. West, 40th Floor
Toronto, Ontario M5H 4E3, Canada
www.Harlequin.com

Printed in U.S.A.

A *USA TODAY* and *Wall Street Journal* bestseller, **Robin Covington** loves to explore the theme of fooling around and falling in love in her books. A Native American author of color, Robin proudly writes diverse romance where everyone gets their happily-ever-after.

She Is an unapologetic comic book geek and hoards red nail polish and stalks Chris Evans. She is thoroughly obsessed with her Corgi, Dixie Joan Wilder (yes—*the* Joan Wilder).

Drop her a line at robin@robincovingtonromance.com— she always writes back.

Find out everything about Robin at her website (robincovingtonromance.com), follow her on Instagram (robincovington), Twitter (@robincovington) and like (really, It's love) her Facebook page.

From Harlequin Desire

Redhawk Reunion

Taking on the Billionaire
Seducing His Secret Wife

Visit her Author Profile page at Harlequin.com, or robincovingtonromance.com, for more titles.

You can also find Robin Covington on Facebook, along with other Harlequin Desire authors, at Facebook.com/harlequindesireauthors!

To Melissa Dark.
You were there at the beginning.
Ten years ago we started this dream together
and I know that I wouldn't be here without you.
Thank you so much. Xoxo

One

Las Vegas, Nevada

There wasn't much in the world that could lure Justin Ling away from a poker table.

He loved the game. The strategy and the psychology and the emotion evoked with every hand that was dealt. It didn't hurt that he'd won far more than he'd ever lost. But he didn't need the money; he was a billionaire from the success of his company, Redhawk/Ling, so winning was a lucrative but empty victory. The upside was that he'd won enough to score invites to some of the largest private games and several of the popular public tournaments. Justin loved the game and when he earmarked weekends to devote to it there was almost nothing that was going to distract him from the cards in his hand.

That's why he couldn't explain why he was sitting down next to the sexy raven-haired beauty at the bar.

She was tall, slim and the kind of sexy that came from a confidence that ran deeper than the superficial trappings of a pair of high heels and makeup. This woman was the kind who made you work for it.

On a break from his current game, he'd seen her walk past the private rooms and head toward the lobby of the casino. And she'd seen him, too. It was a lightning strike of a moment when their eyes locked for several seconds, and the recognition of a reciprocal spark of sexual hunger was enough to find him cashing out and following her into this sad little bar.

"Can I buy you a drink?" He wasted no time getting to the point. Justin always went for what he wanted and this woman had captivated him.

She glanced over at him, giving him a thorough perusal from his toes to his four-hundred-dollar haircut. Her gaze lingered on his face and he thought he saw another flicker of interest in her espresso-colored eyes, but her expression gave nothing away before she turned to watch the football game on the TV at the back of the bar.

"I can buy my own drink." She picked up one of the three shots in front of her and downed it in one quick swallow.

"I'm sure you can," he answered, mirroring her

position on his bar stool with his eyes mostly on the game. He eyed her in his peripheral vision, noting the way she tensed but also noting that she didn't make a move to leave or to tell him to get lost. It gave him encouragement. "In fact, I think *you* should buy *me* a drink."

A few beats of time passed, ratcheting his heart rate up a notch or two when the silence stretched out a little longer than comfortable. He wondered if he'd miscalculated the edge of challenge he'd glimpsed in the way she walked, the strength he'd seen flash in her eyes. If he'd been a betting man, and he was, he'd have all his money on her taking the bait.

And then she laughed.

It wasn't a giggle or a belly laugh. Her lips curved in a sexy twist and the low, husky rumble in her chest made him immediately think of Kathleen Turner, the finest aged whiskey, and secrets whispered in the dark and lost in the folds of tumbled sheets. He turned to face her, unable to resist the need to see her, to witness how the light played across her features and the glossy strands of her hair.

"Are you laughing at me?" he asked, feigning offense as he joined her in chuckling. "I could be offering to use my last twenty to buy you a beverage."

She snorted then and threw in an eye roll for good measure before reaching out and tapping his watch. "This is a Rolex Cosmograph Daytona 40mm. You can afford to buy this bar, so I'm not worried about cleaning out your bank account with an on-tap special."

Damn. His mystery lady had taken the bait, but the only one on the hook was him.

"How do you know so much about watches? Are you a jeweler?" Justin leaned on the bar to move in a little close and didn't even try to keep the impressed tone out of his voice.

She waved a hand in dismissal. "Paul Newman had one just like that and he wore it when he raced cars. I don't know jack about watches but I know cars."

Okay. This woman just got better and better and he had no choice but to keep wading into the deep end even though it looked like she wasn't going to throw him a life raft.

"I'm Justin—"

She shook her head. "I don't do last names."

Fine. If that was how she wanted it. It was how he usually liked it, too. He stuck his hand out.

"Okay, then. I'm just Justin."

She eyed his hand for a minute, an eyebrow raised with a mocking skepticism that took him back to high school and his ill-fated attempts to get the attention of Brandilynn Post, the head cheerleader. Obviously a crash and burn he'd not forgotten, but there'd been a million head cheerleaders in his bed since then and he wasn't scared off by a woman making him earn her attention. With all the women who normally threw themselves at him, this was an exciting change and one that had him hot and intrigued. He knew that if this night ended with her under him, she'd be magnificent.

"I'm Harley." She grasped his hand but instead of lingering on the handshake her long fingers traced along his palm to blatantly examine his ring finger. Now it was his turn to raise his eyebrow in question. She released his hand and shrugged. "Just checking. I'm not into married guys."

"You're assuming that I'm *into* you."

"We both know you are…" she said, taking a sip from her beer before giving him a lingering, hot look that had him shifting even closer. Close enough to feel the silk of her ink-black hair as it brushed against his face. Close enough to see a tiny scar that cut through the outer part of her perfectly arched left eyebrow. He took it as a good sign when she didn't move away and knew it for a fact when she continued, "…and for the moment, *you interest me.*"

Bingo. Justin barely repressed the grin that plucked at the corners of his mouth. He shifted on his bar stool with a pool of fire settling in his groin and making him hard. But while she was currently into him, everything about Harley screamed that she was an untamed filly, ready to bolt at the whisper of anything she didn't like. He wanted to lean over and kiss her but he glanced down at the bar in between them to resist the urge, deciding to circle back to the beginning of this adventure.

"Okay then, can I buy you a drink *now*?"

She picked up the second shot and drank it down. "I'll buy. You need to catch up."

She signaled to the bartender for three shots and motioned for them to be placed in front of him.

Justin picked up the first one, pausing before he put it to his lips. "Are we celebrating something?"

Harley cocked her head to the side, considering the question for a long moment before picking up her remaining shot and tapping it lightly against his own. "Freedom. New beginnings."

· "Whoever he is, he's an idiot." Because the man who'd let this woman slip through his fingers had to be the dumbest man on the planet. Well, the second dumbest... Justin wasn't going to keep her, either. He wasn't deluding himself that what was happening here was a love match or anything.

The vodka burned as it went down; it wasn't as smooth as the brand he normally bought but any criticism disappeared with the chaser of the second shot. He shook his head a little, eyes watering as the alcohol took the first hit at his system and created a slow burn under his skin.

When his vision cleared, Harley was staring at him, her own gaze filled with a different kind of heat, a spark of something. She licked her lips, the universal symbol that she liked what she saw. He found himself back on familiar ground but he braced himself for the moment when she'd knock him off his feet. It wasn't a position he was used to being in with women, but he enjoyed the push and pull with Harley. It was different…more alive and more real than the usual games he played before taking a woman to bed.

"So, who's the guy?" Justin surprised himself with the question. What did he care about the dumb guy who'd let her go? He wasn't interested in the past or the future, just the right now. And unless the loser who'd lost Harley was walking into the bar at this minute to get her back, he didn't care.

But he didn't take back the question, either. Justin wanted to know everything.

Harley cut him a sly look, clearly amused by his curiosity. "His name was Sam. He wanted a commitment that I wasn't ready to make."

Well, that sounded familiar.

"Not ready to commit to him? Or anyone?"

"I think that settling down with someone for the long term is extremely overrated." Justin didn't hide his surprise at her words and so she continued with a tease and tug at the lapel of his jacket. "Whoa. Did I just morph into your dream girl?" She slid her fingertips over his jacket, tugging him closer as she ticked off her list. "No commitments. Can hold her liquor. Likes cars."

Justin grasped her hand and got even closer, mur-

muring against her ear. She shivered a little and he smiled at the reaction. "If you tell me that sex is your favorite indoor activity, I might just have to marry you."

Harley froze for a moment and he felt the jump and stutter of her pulse under his lips. But in a flash she pushed him away and picked up her beer, taking a drink before leveling him with a glare that had more sizzle in it than censure.

"And you had to go and ruin it with the *M* word." She gestured toward his last glass. "Take your penalty shot."

He did as he was told, hooking his foot under the rung of her bar stool and easing her closer as he swallowed the liquid fire. "Is Harley your real name?"

She rested her right elbow on the bar, angling her body into the curve of his own. It was intimate, a mirror of his own posture, and he wondered if she knew she was doing it.

"It's a nickname. I like to restore old cars and bikes. I ride a 1975 Harley."

That was an answer he wasn't expecting. "You're a mechanic?"

"I'm between jobs right now. Taking some time to see this part of the world before I make any plans." Her vague nonanswer was delivered with enough finality that he knew it was nonstarter. But she intrigued him and he wanted to know more about her, so he decided to change tack.

"What's the last song you listened to on your phone?"

The change in topic threw her for a minute but she recovered quickly. "'Jolene' by Ray LaMontagne."

"Nice. Moody and soulful but also very sexy. It suits you," he commented, signaling for another round from the bartender after Harley gave a nod of agreement.

"Okay, now you. Last song," she prompted, as they both tipped back a shot.

Justin hesitated, remembering what he'd been listening to when he'd pulled into valet parking. Oh hell. This is what he got for letting his nephew program playlists into his account. "'Cool' by the Jonas Brothers."

"I don't even want to know what that song says about you." She grimaced and eased a shot glass closer to him. "I think you need to drink to make up for that terrible musical choice."

He paid his penalty, wiping his mouth with comic exaggeration that made her laugh. Damn, but he loved that sound and it made him wonder how her husky tone would wrap around a moan of pleasure. Justin reached down and tangled his fingers with hers, giving them a squeeze of encouragement. "Your turn."

Harley pondered a moment and then said, "Okay, beach or the mountains?"

"That's easy. I'm a California boy. Beaches." He

held up his hand to stop her from answering and then reached out to skim the hair off her face and let the silky strands cool his skin, savoring the slow burn this woman stoked in him. "Let me guess for you."

"Take your best shot."

Justin's fingertips lightly stroked the smooth golden line of her cheekbone and down along her jawline until his hand curled behind her neck and pulled her closer. Harley eased into him, one leg sliding in between his own and her hand resting on his thigh. She was close enough for him to count her long lashes and to feel the fluttering beat of her pulse point. To hear the catch of her breath and the stifled moan of her desire.

Or was that his own?

He leaned in close, his lips brushing against her ear and body pressed against the length of her. Somehow they had ended up in alignment, mirrors of each other except for the brushes of knees, hands and feet. He was hard, every part of him yearning, aching to strip her down and discover all of her secrets. Not just the curve of her body, not just the places that made her want and need—he wanted to know it all.

But he'd start with her in his bed. Under him. Around him.

"Mountains."

"Lucky guess."

Harley shifted, moving just enough to look him in the eye, her mouth only a moment of bravery away from his own. Her eyes were dark, pupils blown with her desire and burning into his with focus flecked with flickers of doubt. Justin wondered what side would win, knowing with every fiber of his being that this had to be her choice. It was her move to make and he was helpless to do anything but wait and see if she would fold or bet it all on one night.

"Ask me what you really want to know," she whispered, biting her lower lip and then running her tongue over the plumpness left behind.

"Will you let me kiss you?"

Her answer was unexpected and exactly what he wanted. Her mouth on his own, soft but not tentative. It told him what he needed to know—that she wanted this, too. That she wanted him. Justin wove his fingers into her hair, anchoring her in place when he increased the pressure, his tongue against the seam of her lips, begging permission to enter and taste her secrets.

Harley's fingers curled around his lapel as she took over the kiss, slanting her mouth over his and opening to entice him inside. They both groaned and he took what he wanted, took what he needed, but it wasn't enough to quench the craving she'd ignited in him.

He pulled her into his lap, balancing both their weights as she straddled him on the stool. Justin's hands shifted, lifting her under her ass cheeks and pressing her against his achingly hard shaft through his pants. She wrapped her arms around his neck, her own desperate need to be closer evidenced by the scrape of her nails against his skin. The pain was good, just enough to ignite his lust to where it was flash point along his veins.

Harley broke away for air and he took the moment to get the answer he needed before they went any further.

Justin couldn't bear to break the connection, so he murmured his question against her mouth, their eyes locked and focused on each other. "Tell me what you want."

"I want you."

It wasn't the first time Justin had woken up in a strange hotel room.

He loved to travel, for business or pleasure, so it wasn't uncommon for him to awaken in a room and have to take a moment to recall the facts, the details of what VIP suite he was in in what VIP city. It also wasn't uncommon for him to wake up with a woman in his bed whom he desperately wanted to leave as soon as possible. But he couldn't remember a time when he'd woken up alone and regretted that a woman left in the middle of night.

Well, there was a first time for everything.

Harley was gone. Like a figment of his imagination or the silky remnant of a dream that he desperately tried to hold on to but couldn't solidify into a memory. Justin knew she had been real. The ache of his body and the scent of her, of them, of sex, lingered on his skin and on the tangle of sheets bunched around his waist.

He eased out of bed, grabbing his discarded pants and slipping them on as he navigated the detritus of their amazing night together flung all over the space of the penthouse suite: empty glasses and bottles on the floor alongside the remnants of an early-morning room service order of celebratory steak and lobster.

And…her wedding veil.

Justin leaned over, his throbbing head immediately signaling to him that it was the worst idea he'd ever had, and his stomach rumbled in ominous, queasy agreement. The veil was one of those cheap ones sold by every wedding chapel on the Strip. Harley had taken her time choosing it, laughing as she attempted to find one that matched her black leather pants and gray T-shirt. When she'd slipped it on, the combination of sex-on-wheels and virginal sacrifice had decimated what had been left of his very iffy mind and he'd marched down the aisle and said two words he'd never planned on saying in his life: "I do."

What had he been thinking? Nothing. That much was clear. He wasn't reckless but he was a risk-taker, never one to shy away from something just because the payoff wasn't guaranteed. It had served him well in business; he could run numbers better than anyone and he'd made himself and a lot of other people a metric ton of money. But nothing was a sure thing and he made people nervous, people who only liked to play it safe, people who hesitated to work with Redhawk/Ling because they couldn't pin him down.

People like the investor group currently considering partnering with the company and giving them the ability to branch out even bigger than they thought possible.

The people who would have a coronary if they heard what he'd done here last night.

He'd gone to Vegas for a poker game and married a complete stranger.

A stranger who had left in the middle of the night.

Justin knew what he had to do. He needed to find this woman and get this marriage dissolved before the press found out and filled every news outlet with another story about his wild and reckless ways. Adam, his best friend and partner in Redhawk/Ling, was going to be pissed. Just last week he'd pleaded with Justin to lie low, to keep his profile more on the respectable side until they'd secured this investment deal and solidified their financial status in the eyes of potential partners. Justin had agreed and he'd kept his end of the bargain.

Until Harley.

And now he had to do damage control, find his wife and keep it out of the press.

He was a gambling man, and he didn't like his odds.

Two

One week later

This had been a mistake.

Sarina Redhawk stood on the deck of her older brother's house counting down the seconds until she could leave and head back to her hotel. In front of her, a crowd of people she didn't know ate barbecue and kept the bartenders occupied pouring fruity drinks while the guests placed their vote in either the blue box with a big bow on top or the pink box with a big bow on top. She'd dropped her ticket in the blue box under the incredibly insistent watch and instruction of someone called Nana Orla.

Adam's house was nice, not Kardashian massive

but large enough to ensure that everyone knew that he
was one of the top tech billionaires in Silicon Valley.
It had been professionally decorated, that was obvious, in bachelor-chic style but personal photographs,
quirky artwork and splashes of color against the neutral sofas and such testified to the entrance of the fiery
redhead into her brother's life. Tess wasn't timid, she
stood tall next to her brother, and Sarina liked her for
it. Adam had chosen well, that much was clear.

Just behind her the canyon spread out beneath
the deck and dipped into deep purple shadows that
reminded her of faraway places she'd served in the
army, places that gave her memories that would always follow her no matter how many oceans and
miles she put between them. But those memories had
taken a back seat lately to the ones she'd been too
young to remember, the ones re-created for her and
contained in the package her brother Adam had given
her and her twin, Roan, when he'd found them again.

Twenty-five years, seven crappy foster homes,
one shitty adoptive home, one GED, one enlistment
and two tours in the Middle East later and she was
here: at the gender reveal party for her older brother
Adam and his fiancée, Tess.

And completely out of her comfort zone.

She'd agreed to come to the party tonight because
she felt bad about storming out of here the last time,
repaying Adam and Tess's hospitality with hostility
and painful words. She hadn't meant to hurt him

but playing "happy family" with two brothers who were essentially strangers had been beyond her ability at the time.

She'd left that night, hopped on her Harley-Davidson and headed straight out of California, needing to put as much distance as she could between her guilty conscience and Adam and Roan's pleas for her to give them all a chance. She'd ignored Adam's voice mails and dodged Roan's FaceTime requests for a couple of months, taking her bike to every small-town, forgotten, one-stoplight spot on the map, enjoying the freedom of choosing her own path for the first time in her life.

She'd been a military policeman in the army and had liked her job but she'd hit the time when she'd had to get out or stay in until retirement. And she'd opted to get out, explore and figure out who the hell Sarina Redhawk was supposed to be when she grew up. She'd thought it would be scary but it had been amazing. Freedom. Time to think. Space to figure some crap out.

Sarina had camped in Tonopah, hung out with Area 51 enthusiasts in Rachel and explored caves in the Great Basin National Park. In the pretty town of Austin, Nevada, she'd found a stray dog outside her hotel and adopted the little Chihuahua, naming her Wilma, and then headed for Las Vegas. She wasn't much of a gambler but she'd picked up some work from an old army buddy for some extra cash while she figured out if she was ever going to answer her brother's phone calls and what she was going to do with the rest of her life.

Las. Fucking. Vegas.

Bright lights. The Blue Man Group. Five ninety-nine steak buffets. The scene of the best night and worst morning after in her life. Sarina had met a man so sexy in the casino bar that she'd violated her newly established rules to not hook up with guys she met in bars. But his smile had been intriguing, his focus unrelenting and their chemistry so explosive that she'd woken up the next morning naked, hungover and very much married. She'd taken one look at the sleeping man in the bed and the simple gold band on her finger and thrown on her clothes faster than tourists snapped up tickets to see the Britney Spears show.

Then she'd done what she did best: she ran. Right back to California to figure how to track down her husband and fix that colossal mistake. And to make amends with Adam and Roan.

And that was why she was at this party. Saying she was sorry for walking out on them before. Trying. It wasn't easy for her to open up to new people, and despite their shared DNA, they were strangers to each other.

Sarina watched Adam and Roan from across the room as they laughed together with Tess. Both men were slender and tall, but Adam was broader in the shoulders and Roan wore his hair long and halfway down his back. If you watched them closely, they had some of the same mannerisms and expressions, the proof that DNA did not lie.

Roan was a successful artist, his star on the rise. He was often in the tabloids, either due to his break-out talent or his revolving bedroom door that admitted both women and men. He was charismatic and outgoing, and drew everyone to him like he invented gravity. Adam was as successful but leaned into the strong, broody and silent vibe to command a room. It didn't surprise anyone that he'd been on the most eligible billionaire tech wiz list for the last decade.

And here Sarina was. Strong and capable—give her a firearm or a mountain to climb and she was the girl. But she was always an outsider; her super-power was knowing when to leave. The hard part was figuring out how to stay.

And figuring out how to ask for help.

Now that the panic had worn off, she had no idea how to find the husband she'd left behind in Vegas. So, she was going to toast her brother's new family tonight and tomorrow she was going to take him up on his offer to help her get her new life started. How surprised was he going to be to find that the first thing she needed was to locate a husband she had no intention on keeping?

Fun times.

"Everybody make sure to cast your vote for the gender of the baby," Nana Orla admonished the crowd in her delightful Irish accent. She was small and smiling but clearly a force of nature because nobody ignored her. Sarina smiled in spite of herself; the army had master sergeants who wished they had the command that she had. "Come in closer, everyone! Move in closer for the big moment!"

Sarina moved with the swell of the crowd, keeping to the outer edge of the mass of bodies but close enough to see the secret smiles and laughter Adam and Tess shared as they moved into place. Always touching in some way, there was no doubt about how much they loved each other. Sarina had been excited to hear about their engagement. She'd liked Tess from the first time they'd met when her future sister-in-law had tracked her down for Adam. She was a straight shooter, strong and smart. The perfect partner for Adam.

And now they were going to be parents and she was going to be an aunt.

Things were changing, and she had no idea where she belonged.

But it was time to figure it out.

Nana Orla summoned everyone closer for the long-awaited moment. People jostled against one another to get in closer to the happy couple and Sarina was suddenly thrust forward into the middle of the group, mumbling her apologies for the elbows jabbed into people's sides and drinks sloshed to the point of spilling. No one seemed to mind—it was a party and they were ready to forgive. She tried to squeeze in between a laughing couple and had to sidestep into a hard, tall body to avoid an elbow to the face. Another shuffle to keep her balance and she stepped onto the foot that belonged to the hard, tall body as did the hands that grasped her hips to keep her upright.

"I'm sorry."

"I've got you," the man said, his voice deep and smooth and interwoven with a thread of humor that had her lips curving into an involuntary smile.

She chuckled, memories of a night full of laughter and passion coming back with the impact of muscle memory. Her reaction was visceral, immediately sending warmth and heat along her skin. How many times had she shivered from the sizzle of just the memory of that night, craved the touch of the stranger she'd left in that bed?

It wasn't new.

Wait.

The voice wasn't new.

The man wasn't a stranger.

Sarina twisted away from the man, braced herself for what she knew was coming and looked up into the face of her husband.

The ground beneath her feet shifted, the room suddenly becoming too hot and the crowd unbearably close. She braced herself for impact, her body knowing full well what was coming even if her brain wasn't there yet.

"What the hell are you doing here?" she demanded, noticing the curious looks of the people immediately around them.

"Me? What about you?" the man replied in a hushed tone, his eyes scouring her face with eager curiosity and hunger that she knew all too well. It had been like this from the first, some unexplainable heat that sparked between them like electricity trying to complete the arc.

Justin. He'd said his name was Justin.

"Justin, right? What the hell? This doesn't make sense," she sputtered, chasing her erratic thoughts around like a dropped bag of marbles. "What are you doing in my brother's house?"

"Your what…brother?" Justin said, shaking his head as if to dislodge whatever was stuck in there. "The name on the marriage license is Sarah Moore…"

"It's my adopted name," she answered, holding her hand up to stop him from asking new questions before she got answers to her own. "Are you going to tell me why you're in Adam's house?"

"He's my best friend, my business partner. I'm Justin Ling." He gestured with his hands between himself and Adam standing a few feet away. "I'm the Ling part of Redhawk/Ling." He scrubbed a hand over his face, gazing up at the ceiling in disbelief with what looked a lot like disgust. "Not only did I marry a stranger, she turns out to be my best friend's little sister."

Sarina opened her mouth to tell him to keep his voice down but she was interrupted by a loud countdown from the crowd, and both she and Justin turned to watch as Adam and Tess pulled the string on the box in front of them. A huge bouquet of blue balloons sprang out of the box and shot to the ceiling.

"It's a boy!"

"Congrats!"

Applause rang out around them, loud and disorienting, as everyone around her toasted the new parents, completely oblivious to the shitstorm she had created with the man standing by her side. Life had a way of messing with you and right now she knew she was solidly in its crosshairs.

"It's a boy!" rose up again from somewhere behind her as she raised her eyes to the handsome face of the stranger she'd married.

She almost laughed at the ridiculousness of this moment, but it wasn't that funny. While Adam and Tess were celebrating the imminent arrival of their bouncing baby boy, she'd just been handed a sexy-as-hell, six-foot-something bundle of holy-shit-I-married-a-stranger-in-Vegas.

It was a boy all right.

What was she going to do with him?

Three

Adam was going to kill him.

Justin glanced over to where his best friend and business partner was kissing his fiancée and accepting the congratulations from the crowd assembled here to celebrate the biggest event of his life.

Well, the biggest event if you didn't count the recent discovery of Adam's long-lost siblings.

So, the fact that Justin had gone to Vegas, gotten ridiculously drunk with an incredibly captivating stranger and married her was bad enough. But the fact that the mesmerizing, mind-blowing, amazing woman turned out to be Adam's baby sister?

Justin. Was. A. Dead. Man.

He raked his eyes around the space for somewhere

he could grab a minute of privacy with his newly sur-
faced wife. They had a lot to talk about.

Like why the hell she'd left that morning and
where the hell she'd been.

"Come with me." Justin took Sarina's hand and
guided her through the crowd, headed straight for
Adam's office. He knew this house as well as he
knew his own, and that room would be safe from
curious partygoers.

"Where are we going?" Sarina asked behind him,
her voice steely with warning that she was going to
give him a little bit of rope and then she'd string him
up with it if he didn't get to the point.

In spite of the absolute insanity of this moment, he
caught himself smiling. It was her backbone, her direct
promise to call him on his bullshit that had intrigued
Justin back in that Vegas bar. People didn't call him
on much—either because of his money or his family's
position in society—and he liked that she didn't care.

The Lings were big money, and had even bigger
social prominence in this part of California, his father a self-made man in real estate and his mother
the queen of the fundraising committees. Justin, even
with a billion-dollar company with his name on the
door, was the runt of the over-achieving Ling litter.
His siblings were upstanding members of the community while Justin gambled and had a revolving
bedroom door and refused to even play Putt-Putt at
the country club.

He bet that Sarina played a mean game of miniature golf.

"Hello? Where are we going?" she insisted, balking at being dragged across the room with no explanation.

"To Adam's office. We can get some privacy in there," he answered, feeling the acquiescence in her grip on his hand as they navigated the bodies in the crowd. Once he reached the large double doors, he opened them and drew her inside. The immediate impact of blocking out the swell of voices was enough to disorient him for a few seconds.

Or maybe it was the woman standing before him.

She was tall, only a few inches shorter than his six feet two inches, muscular, slim, with straight hair the color of black licorice down to her shoulders. Her eyes were the deepest brown with flecks of bronze and her face was cut glass, angles etched in amber.

Sarina was stunning.

And he was staring and holding her hand like a kid who'd just figured out that girls were hot.

The only consolation was that she was staring right back at him, heat answering heat. The pull from that night was back, leaving no question about how they'd ended up in this mess.

Hormones. Chemistry. It was as simple and hard and confusing and amazing as that.

Justin let go of her hand, his body singing in protest at the break in the connection. He stalked around the room, needing the activity to think this through. There were so many moving parts to this catastrophe but he could figure it out. He'd bashed through other barriers, done stuff that nobody thought he could accomplish. He was the kid that nobody thought would make it and he'd figured out how to fight to make sense of stuff that came so easy to other people. He'd become an expert at solving problems. This was just another puzzle to solve, right?

"So, you're Adam's business partner?" Sarina asked, her expression dark with a healthy dose of confused thrown into the mix. She wasn't any happier about this than he was. "Does he know about…"

"About our getting hitched? Nope. I just got back to town a couple of days ago and I was trying to figure out how to deal with it without getting him involved." Justin paused, recollecting one pertinent fact that might be the solution to their problem. "Wait. You married me under a fake name. That must mean that our marriage is invalid."

She shook her head, her hand slashing across the air between them. "Not fake. *Adopted.* I'm in the middle of getting my name officially changed back to Sarina Redhawk but Sarah Moore is my name… for now."

"They didn't let you keep any part of your given name? Adam's adoptive parents let him keep his name," he said, realizing too late that he was probably not telling her anything she didn't know.

"Well, that was mighty nice of them, wasn't it? I guess it made them feel better about taking a kid from a perfectly happy family and erasing every piece of his heritage from his life. I'll make sure they get a prize."

Sarina did nothing to cloak the bitterness in her words and it was so potent that even he tasted the acrid taste of the betrayal. Justin had sat through many long talks with Adam over the years, wishing he could do something to help him, and this moment with Sarina was no different. He didn't know the details of her life—they weren't Adam's to tell—but Justin knew that Adam's younger siblings hadn't had easy lives.

Unfairly taken from their family by the state when Adam was six years old and the twins, Sarina and Roan, were three, they'd been shipped off to families in separate parts of the country. Adam had hired Tess to find them as soon as he had the means, a search that had resulted in their reunion several months earlier. It wasn't the happy event that Adam had envisioned, and Justin had ached for his friend. A quintessential first-born, Adam wanted to take care of everyone and it killed him that the pain of his siblings' lives wasn't something he could just fix with a wave of his hand.

Adam and Roan were making progress in their relationship but Adam had relayed that his sister had been angry, unwilling to even give it a try. She'd been through too much... They'd all been through too much.

"Yeah, Adam's family isn't great," Justin said, knowing that it was the worst of understatements but it also wasn't the point right this minute. Any minute now they could be interrupted, and they needed to figure some stuff out first. "But right now we have more pressing matters to worry about. No matter what your name is legally, we've got to figure out a way to end this marriage as quickly and as quietly as possible."

"Agreed. How do we do that?" Sarina asked, one hand on her hip, the other making the speed-it-up motion in the air.

Justin bit back a laugh. She was snarky and prickly but he thought it was sexy as hell. He was pretty sure that telling her that right now would end in his death, so he kept his mouth shut.

"What the hell is going on? What marriage?"

Justin and Sarina both jumped at the sound of Adam's voice, pivoting to take in the figures of Adam and Tess standing in the open office doorway. Sounds from the party drifted into the space, disguising Justin's muttered "oh, shit" as he motioned them inside the room. So much for breaking it to Adam at the right time and place, and forget not telling him at all.

He looked at Sarina, knowing her irritated but resigned expression was echoed by his own. Finally, she lifted a shoulder in a shrug that said it all: it was what it was. It wasn't going to get any better. They needed to just get it over with.

Justin took a deep breath and faced his best friend, unconsciously moving closer to his wife as he broke the news. Maybe they weren't destined for a ruby wedding, but they were in this together for now.

"This isn't how we wanted to tell you…"

"I didn't want to tell you at all," murmured Sarina.

"That, too." Justin's lips twitched in a smile in spite of the seriousness of the situation. Sarina was a badass with a really twisted, dark sense of humor. He liked her. A lot. "When I went to Vegas last week I met Sarina at the casino…"

"You were at that high-roller poker game last week," Adam interrupted, his brow creased in confusion. "How…?"

"They don't tie us to the tables, man," Justin said, rushing into the next part. "I met Sarina and we hung out and got married."

It was overly simplistic and left out a shit ton of details, but did it really matter?

Apparently it did.

"How the hell do you go to Vegas and end up married to my sister?" Adam asked, not quite yelling but pretty damn close.

Justin really didn't want to go into the how and why of the entire night. Not when he couldn't remember all of it. But Sarina had no qualms about it. The brutal honesty he'd admired a few moments earlier was less appealing at the moment.

"Adam, it's not that hard to figure out," she said, her expression daring him to call her on any of this. "We met in a bar, got drunk, and woke up the next morning covered in glitter and in possession of a marriage license. I had no idea who he was."

"I've only ever seen pictures of her as a child, Adam. I had no idea she had a different name." Justin filled in his part of the story, hurrying to explain the insanity.

Adam's mouth fell open and Tess grabbed on to his arm in an attempt to calm him down. Justin wasn't worried—Adam wasn't the kind of guy who punched first and asked questions later. But Justin had never married his sister before, so there was always room for error.

"Justin, did you *sleep* with my sister?"

"Adam." Tess groaned at the question, flashing Sarina an apologetic look and Justin a lift of the eyebrows as if to say *really*.

Sarina wasn't having any part of it, either. "Nope. We're not going there. I wasn't some innocent virgin lured over to the dark side. I was a fully participating *adult* in all activities including the marriage part and the *sex* part…which was great, by the way."

"Agreed," Justin couldn't resist adding at the look of horror on Adam's face. It really wasn't funny but the alternative was facing up to the fact that he'd fucked up again and was living up to his reckless reputation. Adam was too shocked to be pissed right now but his anger when it came would be well deserved. Justin had one job and he'd messed up big time.

"No. No," Adam spat out, his hands shooting up in a gesture meant to ward off all mention of his sister's sex life.

Tess jumped in, stifling a laugh as she steered the conversation back to the heart of the matter. "So what are you two going to do about the marriage? Are you going to stay together or what?"

"No," they both replied in unison, their gazes pulled together in a search for confirmation. The impact of the moment shook Justin again, as he felt the same connection, the same spark, the same flood of memories of smooth naked skin and hot, sweet kisses traded in the midst of tangled sheets.

His mind knew that he needed to end this marriage. His body said that he needed to get her back in his bed and indulge until he was ready to move on like he always did. His gut said that he'd be hard-pressed to find someone it was so easy to laugh with and talk to. Sarina had gotten him from the first moment.

Damn.

Sarina's cheeks pinkened and she blinked hard, breaking the connection with a sharp turn of her body away from him and several steps in the opposite direction. Justin fought the urge to go over to her but they didn't need to complicate this, especially since she'd still be in his life after this marriage was over because she was Adam's sister. Damn, this was tricky.

"Justin, I don't need to tell you how bad this would be if it got out in the press," Adam continued, oblivious to the undercurrent pulsing between the two of them. "We have the chance to partner with Aerospace Link. This is huge."

Sarina turned to face them with a confused expression, and Justin filled her in. "Aerospace Link is the largest satellite company in the world and it's still a family business. They are pretty old-school and have expressed hesitation at some of my lifestyle choices."

Sarina shook her head in confusion. "Your private life isn't part of the deal. One is business and one isn't."

"When you're asking people who've invested billions in a joint venture to trust a company that's a relative infant in the tech industry to deliver what we promise, the behavior of the guy who runs the financial end of the business is part of the deal," Justin explained. "If they can't trust me, they can't trust Redhawk/Ling."

"They act like he's the poster child for *Billionaires Gone Wild* and aren't thrilled that the CFO of our company spends a lot of time on the front page of tabloids," Adam added, his tone protective of Justin. It was a familiar theme of their friendship; Justin had been the black sheep of his family and Adam was his biggest cheerleader.

Justin appreciated it but he couldn't let Adam downplay the truth of the headlines. "I like women and parties and high-stakes poker games," he explained with unapologetic honesty. "But I don't gamble with company money and I'm a damn good CFO. Numbers are the easiest thing in the world to me and I can sniff out a turn in the market faster than anyone else. I'm not interested in letting them dictate my personal life, but I have to agree that getting married while drunk in Vegas isn't a great thing to put on my résumé and is a legitimate reason for them to question the stability of Redhawk/Ling."

"So dissolving this marriage needs to stay off the front page," Sarina stated, her expression reading more exasperated than confused.

"It needs to stay off *any* page, or Aerospace Link will back out and other partners and investors will wonder why. Big business leaders talk to each other and we'll be loath to find anyone who'll want to do business with Redhawk/Ling. This could be a long-term disaster for us," Justin said, flashing a look of regret at Adam. Once again he was a disappointment to the people in his life. "I'm sorry, Adam."

His best friend waved off his apology, his expression kind as usual. They'd been through a lot together, supported each other through the worst and celebrated each other through the best. It would take more than this to make Adam Redhawk turn his back on him, but sometimes Justin wondered where the line was and when he would cross it.

"Justin, you didn't do this by yourself." Sarina's voice was firm and clear across the room. She walked over, stopping to stand shoulder to shoulder with him to face her brother. "And I don't want to be part of the reason Redhawk/Ling suffers."

She didn't reach out to touch him but there was no doubt that she was in this with him, that she was here for the long haul. Justin recalled that she had been in the army and her body language was the definition of loyalty born from a shared experience in the trenches. This situation wasn't ideal but it would be easier if they weren't at each other's throats.

Justin smiled at her, hoping she read the high level of thanks in the expression before turning back to Adam and Tess. "I'll contact our attorneys to get this wrapped up as quickly and quietly as we can."

Sarina nodded at each of them as she backed away and headed for the door. "So let's recap—we get divorced but keep it off TMZ. Adam and Tess, congratulations on the baby boy. I'm tapped out on family time for now, so I'm going to go."

And just like that morning in Vegas, she was gone.

Justin watched the door shut behind her, admiring her style. It was why they hooked up in the first place and why he couldn't take his eyes off her. Sarina was direct, no-holds-barred and a challenge. Hell, he never could resist a challenge. And Sarina Redhawk was a walking, talking invitation for him to keep making bad choices.

Adam stepped into his field of vision, arms crossed as he glared at him. "Don't think I forgot that you *slept* with my sister."

Justin grinned. What else could he do? "But I married her first. That should be a consolation."

Four

The Valley Hotel was a shithole.

Okay, maybe that was a little bit harsh, but Justin felt like it was one double murder in the parking lot away from being in the category of hotel that was featured prominently on cable television shows with titles that included "unsolved" and "most wanted" and played in constant cycles of syndication. The faux-Spanish, single-story hacienda-style building was old and decaying and had given up a long time ago.

A Silicon Valley landmark it wasn't. He wasn't even sure it passed the fire code. He shuddered when he thought about what a black light would reveal if it was aimed at any surface in this place.

Justin navigated a discarded bag of fast food on the asphalt, narrowly missing stepping in a puddle of spilled milkshake and half a joint. He pulled his phone out of his pocket and tapped the screen to call Adam.

"Adam, do you know where Sarina is staying?" he asked, disgust coating every one of his words. "Why isn't she staying with you?"

A big sigh wafted over the connection and he could picture Adam sitting at his desk, hands reaching for the ever-present drumsticks to tap out his frustration. His buddy was secretly in a band that played at a local dive bar once a month. The members were a group of engineers from Stanford so it wasn't going to hit MTV anytime soon but they were pretty decent and had a rabid following. "Yeah, I do. It's a shithole. She won't stay with me and insists on paying her own bill. I'm not arguing with her about it anymore. It's exhausting."

"You can't let her stay here, Adam. This place is disgusting and very likely dangerous," Justin said as he scanned the room numbers for the correct one. He spied it across the lot and headed over, determined to find Sarina and get her out of here.

"Well, she's *your* wife, Justin. So good luck with that." Adam drawled, his tone more you're-an-idiot and less I'm-going-to-kill-you than it had been since they'd revealed the Vegas wedding to him. It was an improvement. Justin expected him to hang up so the chuckle over the line surprised him. "She was in the military, Justin. Trained in firearms. Be careful that she doesn't shoot you."

The call ended and Justin jammed the phone into his pocket and cursed out his best friend/brother-in-law. Sarina's staying at this place wasn't funny at all. It wasn't safe and she *was* his wife. He wouldn't sleep at night knowing that she was here. He had enough money to buy this hotel about thirty times over and he could pay for her to stay anywhere else. This was unacceptable.

He headed across the lot, growing more determined with each step to get to Sarina's room and get her out of here. Justin stopped at the door to room 18 and knocked, listening for any sign that she was inside. He glanced around the lot, looking for her motorcycle, but it was nowhere in sight. Sarina loved that bike—that was something she'd made clear that first night in Vegas—so its absence didn't bode well.

He heard someone approach the door and he knew that he was being observed through the peephole. He smiled and pointed at the doorknob.

"Let me in. I need to talk to you," he said, relieved when he heard the lock slide inside. The door opened enough for him to see Sarina scowling at him. Her hair was pulled back into a ponytail and she wore no makeup, but he'd never seen a more beautiful woman.

She didn't need any of that stuff his mom and sisters spent hours applying and hundreds of dollars stocking in their larger-than-life bathrooms. Her skin was flawless, a honey-caramel color, black lashes thick and heavy as they lined her deep, expressive brown eyes. Her lips were full even when they pulled tight in a frown, even when her smile only hinted at the plump, sexy pout.

Justin swallowed hard; his first instinct was to lean in, kiss her and claim that mouth just like he had that night in Vegas. He knew how to get that mouth to soften, knew how to coax her into opening to him and letting him take deep, drugging kisses that left them both shaking. Damn, he'd wanted her so much and they'd been combustible in bed. She'd been responsive and demanding and insatiable and completely into him. He'd had a lot of women under him over the years but none of them had left him aching and wanting more like her. It was the best time he'd ever had inside and out of the bedroom.

Sarina had been his match but he'd been too caught up in the maelstrom of passion that night and he'd had no time to overthink it. And the next morning when he'd woken up to her gone he'd experienced a level of disappointment he wasn't accustomed to. There wasn't much in life that Justin wanted that he didn't get. He'd grown up in a wealthy family and now he had his own money, a fortune that put his family's bank account to shame.

"Why are you here, Justin?" Sarina asked, noticeably not inviting him inside. He wasn't surprised; there was nothing easy about her.

"Can I come in? I need to talk to you about the divorce proceedings," he said as he cast a disgusted glance around the hotel. "And we need to talk about your current accommodations."

Her eyebrows shot up at the last part, and then her eyes narrowed into be-careful-what-you-say slits. "Did Adam send you?"

"Nope. In fact, he told me not to waste my time."

"So my brother is smarter than you are. Good to know who the brains and the beauty are in your relationship," she observed, stepping back to let him in the room.

It was as bad as he thought it would be. Shabby carpet and curtains in colors that were muted from sun exposure and many washings. The bed was unmade and there was an overwhelming smell of bleach wafting up from the linens, which made him feel better about the cleanliness of the place. None of it changed his mind about her staying here.

"At least you still think I'm pretty," he joked, scrambling for something to say now that they were alone and face-to-face in this odd place.

Sarina paused in her hurried effort to pick up a jacket thrown over the arm of the only chair in the room. She looked him over, nice and slow, not hiding the heated approval that slid across her expression. "Justin, my thinking you're pretty is how we got in this mess."

And there it was. He moved in closer, so they were standing chest-to-chest, close enough for him to see the flash of humor that battled with the attraction in her eyes.

Close enough to hear her growl.

"Did you just growl at me?" he asked, taking a step back just in case it really was her.

The bedcovers next to him moved and he jumped back, not sure what the hell was going on. The growling got louder as the thing under the covers crept closer and closer to the edge of the bedspread. Then, after much wiggling and growling, a small white fur-covered face appeared in the opening. With teeth bared and long pointy ears projected from each side of its head, it looked like something from a science fiction movie.

"Did you pick up Baby Yoda in Vegas?"

Sarina scoffed, lifting the creature in her arms and cradling it against her chest. It was a little white dog, a Chihuahua with big buggy eyes and wearing a tiny black T-shirt with Lady Gaga on it.

"This is Wilma Mankiller," she said, pressing a kiss to the little head and snuggling her closer. "I found her in a little town in Nevada. She bites."

Justin pulled back his hand, taking Sarina at her word. "That's quite a name. Has she actually killed a man?"

"Not yet," Sarina said, setting her down on the floor and watching as she headed over to a bowl of water. "But she's named after the first woman chief of the Cherokee nation. My Wilma is a badass. She was fighting off a really fat feral cat behind a dumpster at a diner. I had to take her."

"Does this place allow pets?" Justin asked, cringing at the worst segue in history. But he needed to get back to the subject of why she was staying in a dump like this.

Sarina plopped down in the chair. "It does and I can afford it. If you're here to tell me it's not the Ritz-Carlton, I know."

"Sarina, you can't stay here. I can afford to put you up in a much nicer place."

"I don't want your money, Justin. If I won't take Adam's money, why do you think I would take it from you?" Sarina crossed her arms across her chest, signaling that this was going to be a lot harder than he'd predicted. "This place is fine. I shouldn't be here that long. Once we put the marriage in the rearview mirror, I'll be back on the road."

"I heard back from the lawyers this morning and it's going to take six weeks for us to get the marriage dissolved. They think they can get it annulled."

"Six weeks?" Sarina scrunched up her nose in distaste. "I didn't think it took that long."

"Apparently, a quickie wedding doesn't equate to a quickie divorce." He sat down on the edge of the dresser, doling out the less-than-exciting news he'd received this morning. "The lawyers are drawing up the papers and they are contacting the Las Vegas officials to do what they can to keep it quiet. The six-week time frame should coincide perfectly with closing of the Aerospace Link deal so if we can keep it on the down low, it won't impact Redhawk/Ling."

"Well, damn." Sarina shook her head in frustration. "My money is going to run out before that happens." She glanced at Justin. "My bike needs work I can't do myself and I'm bleeding cash on that bill. I'm going to need to find a job to fund the repair and my next road trip. I still haven't made it to the Grand Canyon."

"I can give you the money," Justin said. "It's the least I can do." He knew the minute he said it and her arms crossed her chest that the answer to that offer had not changed. Time to try another option. "Okay, okay. I've got a job for you."

"Sure you do." Sarina scoffed, motioning toward him in a give-it-to-me waggle of her fingers. "Do I look like I was born yesterday?"

"It's a real job, Sarina. I swear." Justin lifted his hand in the Boy Scout pledge, chuckling when Sarina laughed and shook her head in disbelief. "Adam and I started a foundation called Rise Up to offer outreach to kids in the foster system. We provide sports, crafts, music, language lessons, all kinds of things for them. We're still looking for a new full-time director but we need someone to coordinate stuff in the meantime. I figure with your army background, you could do this in your sleep. I know you perfected organization and dealing with people in the service. All I need you to do is organize some activities for the older kids, be a presence at the center, show up for them. This will be a walk in the park."

"Foster kids? Still in the system?" Sarina was interested and he knew enough from her background that she had a lot in common with them. "Private home placement or group home?"

"Both. And these kids are getting ready to age out so we're helping them prepare for it. We offer them some support after they age out, but we can't do it forever."

"It's a hard thing for a kid to face." Sarina considered the offer, reaching down to pick up Wilma and put her on her lap. Her tone remained skeptical but he took it as a good sign that she was still asking questions. "It pays?"

"Enough to get your bike fixed and for you to put some money away for your road trip."

"And this is a real job? Not something made up to just give me a handout?" Sarina was suspicious and direct. "I don't take handouts, Justin. I'm not afraid of hard work but I want to earn what I have."

"Look, while I have enough money to fill your hands and about a million other people's, I respect your need to carry your own weight. *Believe me*, I get it. I wouldn't insult you by making up a job that didn't exist." And he really did get it. Being the black sheep in a family of overachievers wasn't the worst position in the world but it had made him determined to make it on his own. It also made him incredibly stubborn. Justin stood, not ready to take no for an answer. "But I have one condition on the job."

"And what is that?"

He looked around the room and shuddered. "You can't stay at the No-Tell Motel."

"It's fine."

"It's cheap," Justin countered, refusing to leave her here for one more minute. He cast another glance around the room and shuddered. "And terrifying."

Sarina rolled her eyes. "Well, I'm not staying with you."

Justin shook his head. He'd anticipated this. If she wouldn't stay with Adam, she wasn't going to shack up with him. "No. You're going to stay with Nana Orla."

Five

Sarina didn't like to owe anyone.

Justin had helped her pack her few belongings, then bundled her and Wilma into his Porsche 911 Turbo and peeled out of the parking lot so fast she expected to see a zombie horde chasing them in the rearview mirror. She'd debated fighting him on the move but the bottom line was that she couldn't afford to stay at that hotel for six weeks and pay for the repairs on her bike. She had some savings after leaving the army but she'd spent a lot of money on her road trip, and the truth of the matter was that it was flowing out faster than it was flowing in.

She'd spent the morning scouring the want ads for jobs she could walk to or get to by bus. It didn't matter what the job was; she'd done every kind of work there was to put money in her pocket and food on her table. Honest work was honest work. She wasn't too proud to clean a toilet but she was independent.

And while she was currently married to one billionaire and was the younger sister of another, she wasn't ready to lean on them for her livelihood. She'd spent most of her life trying not to owe people anything.

Owing people gave them power over you and while it was a given that everybody had to work for somebody, she wanted to choose who had any control over her life. But she also knew when she had to take what was on offer in order to get back to where she was in control of her life again.

So this job was a lucky break and she'd earn her keep and some cash. She didn't like the condition of accepting a free room but she really didn't have a choice. Justin had been 100 percent correct when he'd said that she'd never get her bike fixed if she had to pay for a room for that long.

This was practical and smart, but she didn't have to like it.

But there was something she needed to clear up first.

"Who is Nana Orla and why is she going to let me stay at her house?"

Justin chuckled, giving her a side-eye glance as he changed lanes. "She's my grandmother on my mother's side. She came over from Ireland when I was five or six years old to live with us. You couldn't have missed her at the party. She's loud and bossy and takes no shit from anyone." He winked at her. "Sound like anyone else I know?"

Sarina ignored him, refusing to be drawn in by his amusing sex appeal. "And why would she let me live with her?"

"Because I'm her favorite."

"Uh-huh."

"True story."

Sarina sneaked a peek at the man she'd married as they drove toward Nana Orla's house. He focused on the road, tapping the steering wheel to the beat of the Red Hot Chili Peppers song pouring out of the speakers, so she took the opportunity to take a longer look.

Justin was still ridiculously hot. Tall and slim, with dark hair and tanned skin, he moved like a man who was in complete control of his life. She'd known he was rich the first minute she'd laid eyes on him. He walked like someone who owned the world around him and could buy several others. Charming and charismatic, his sparkling eyes and contagious smile were the things that drew her to him from jump. Justin was like the pied piper—his sex appeal the only flute he'd needed to entice her to follow him into that wedding chapel.

Yeah, they'd been drunk but she'd married him

because he'd made her feel like she was all he needed. And that was something she hadn't felt in her life. Ever.

And that night in the hotel room had been like nothing she'd ever experienced before. Sarina had never felt so wanted or needed or desired. Sex had always been good. She liked it a lot and never felt ashamed of taking what she wanted. But sex with Justin had been…earth-shattering. So gravity-shifting that she'd felt compelled to run as fast as she could the next morning. And now that she'd found him again it was terrifying that the last thing she wanted to do was run. She wanted to stay. To get to know him better. To satisfy her curiosity and figure out why this man intrigued her.

Which was why she was going to keep as much distance between them as she could until they were no longer bound for better or for worse…richer and poorer wasn't an issue. His bank account testified that money was never a problem for him.

Justin glanced over, catching her in mid-ogle. He lifted his lips in a smirk, his eyes dancing with mischief. "To be honest, I thought you'd fight me more on this."

She chuckled, turning to face the window and watching the scenery change from the Amanda Jones side of the tracks to the Cher Horowitz suburbs. "I'm self-sufficient, not stupid. I need to get my bike fixed."

"And that place was disgusting. Zero stars."

She rolled her eyes. "Justin, I was in the army. Two tours in Afghanistan. I can stay anywhere. I've stayed in places with no heat or running water. My biggest worry was wondering what would have crawled into my clothes during the night."

"Yeah, well," he said, shifting in his seat and clearing his throat. "You don't have to do that anymore."

"Why? Because my brother is rich?" She snorted out a laugh. "Because I married you?"

"Well…yeah." He sounded perplexed, like he didn't understand why she didn't just rush out and buy a Rolex or apply for an American Express Centurion card.

Not gonna happen.

She leaned back in the seat, turning to look at Justin as they navigated the road up into the hills. "Justin, that's not my money. Never has been and never will be. I'm not trying to be mean but that's just the only way this is ever going to be."

"I know you didn't have it easy growing up. I know Adam would like to help you," Justin said.

"What did he tell you about my life?" Sarina asked, her voice harsh with the anger that suddenly erupted in her gut. She sat up, the seat belt pressing against her chest with the sudden movement and slapping her back against the leather seats. "What do you *think* you know?"

Justin jumped in. "Whoa. Adam told me nothing, but I'm his best friend. It didn't take much for me to figure out that wherever you ended up after you guys were taken wasn't great. It upset him. In case you hadn't figured it out, your brother has a huge white knight complex going on. He takes that shit on like it's all his fault. I put two and two together." He cast a meaningful glance in her direction, a mix of confusion and disapproval. He didn't like her thinking poorly of her brother—and his best friend. That was clear. It made her feel good knowing that her brother had this guy in his corner. "Adam would *never* betray you like that. He's the best man I know."

Sarina let that sink in, recalling a similar observation from Adam. "That's funny. He said the same thing about you."

Justin huffed out a laugh. "Was that before or after he found out about Vegas?"

"Both." Sarina shifted the sleeping Wilma on her lap, smiling at the snuffling snores that racked her little body. "Back at the hotel you said you got that I needed to carry my own weight."

"Is there a question in there?" Justin asked, his voice guarded and his body shifting away from her. It was a subtle move but she was hyper-focused on him and didn't miss it. It was a touchy subject for him, so she'd tread carefully.

"Just the obvious one. You grew up rich—"

"And that means I've never had to work for anything? I was handed everything on a silver platter?"

She sighed, realizing that she'd stepped in it. "I'm sorry, that's not what I meant. I'm genuinely curious. I want to know what you meant."

A long silence stretched out between them. Anthony Kiedis sang about a bridge and she settled back in her seat, totally okay with passing the rest of the ride without talking. She'd learned to live in the quiet spaces and the army had exposed her to every kind of person. She didn't take everything personally; just because someone didn't want to share the intimate details of their life with her, it wasn't the end of the world. Justin didn't owe her anything. Especially not an explanation of his life.

If they kept this arm's length, that would be better anyway. Neither of them needed to form an attachment.

"Let's just say that my path to success wasn't the one my parents expected me to take. Compared to my brothers and sisters, I was the intellectual runt of the litter," Justin said, his voice flat with the effort to try not to sound like it mattered. But it was obvious that it mattered…a lot.

"You did okay, *more* than okay," Sarina said, stating the obvious when they were sitting in a car that cost over one hundred thousand dollars.

"I proved what I needed to prove," Justin answered, turning into a driveway framed by a pair of elaborate metal gates. He rolled down the window, keying in a code that opened the gates and let them onto the property. "I never had to prove anything to Nana Orla. She accepted me just the way I was." He flashed her a grin, but Sarina didn't miss the genuine affection in his eyes when he talked about his grandmother. "I *told* you I'm her favorite."

Sarina sat up straighter, the large estate spreading out as far as she could see. Landscaped grounds spilled into water features and orchards that opened up to a majestic Spanish-style manor house that sat nestled into the shelter of the rising hills. She leaned forward, jaw dropping at the sheer mass of the mansion. It looked like something featured on one of the reality TV shows that had nothing to do with actual reality. Instead of pulling up into the circular driveway, Justin followed the road around the mansion, heading past an elaborate garden and pool area straight toward a smaller home set in the middle of a grove of orange trees.

The house was built in the same style of the mansion, but it was much smaller. Large enough to hold a few bedrooms, it was bigger than any house she'd ever lived in. With pots of flowers on each side of the front walk and a hand-painted welcome sign on the door, it was inviting. Staying here would be…nice.

A smaller pool and patio with a firepit and barbecue were nestled next to the house, just beyond the two-car garage. Justin pulled to a stop in front of it, turning off the car and waking up a grumbling Wilma, who growled at the disruption to her nineteen-hour-per-day nap routine. Sarina shushed her, stroking the silky soft fur between her ears and getting a doggy kiss reward.

The interior of the car was quiet but not uncomfortable as they both stared forward. For her part, Sarina was processing all that had happened in the last few days to get her in this spot with this man. She didn't know Justin well enough to know what he was thinking but she could probably guess.

He shifted in his seat to face her and she mirrored his movements. Sarina held her breath, trying to still the flutter of butterflies in her stomach and the race of heat-induced goose bumps on her skin. He smiled, the slow, I-know-how-to-flip-your-world-on-its-head grin that had kept her glued to that bar stool in Vegas and then following him down the path to the altar. It was hard to believe that this man ever had to prove anything to anyone and harder to believe that he might not have measured up.

She wasn't the only one feeling something. Justin swallowed hard, his gaze hot and heavy on her. His focus drifted from her mouth, down to where her breasts pushed against her tank top with the ridiculously fast beat of her heart, and then lifted again to her eyes. Everything from the taut lines of his muscles under his shirt, to the fierce grip of his fingers on his thighs, to his heavy breathing that mirrored her own proved he was right here in this craziness with her. And it scared her to death.

"Sarina…" Justin reached out, his hand sliding over her own, the rough brush of his fingers sparking all of her nerve endings. He leaned in closer, his breath drifting across her cheek, his gaze drifting down to her mouth and back up to her eyes. He wanted to kiss her. She *wanted* him to kiss her. It was a bad idea and she didn't care. "You are trouble."

"I think you *like* a little trouble."

His grin turned sultry and he nodded, leaning in even closer. All she had to do was move forward an inch and she'd be able to taste him again.

A knock on the passenger-side window made them both jump and Wilma barked in warning as she scrambled to lunge at the window. Justin peered over her shoulder, rolling his eyes as he recognized the woman gesturing at them through the glass.

Justin reached over to hit the button to lower the window. "Brace yourself. Nana Orla is one-of-a-kind and we are all thankful for that."

The older woman quickly assessed the situation, the eyebrows raised in disapproval and the hands on her hips testifying that she wasn't going to put up with any nonsense. She spoke in a flurry of words that left Sarina blinking in astonishment.

"Justin, what are you doing sitting in my driveway with a girl? Weren't you raised to bring her inside the house? Where are your manners? It's like that boy that used to pull up and honk for your sister on dates. Disgusting." Nana Orla turned her attention to Sarina, her grin a matching twin to Justin's. "I apologize, love. Raised by wolves, I swear."

Her accent was amazing, full Irish and the kind that made getting chewed out a pure pleasure.

"Here, give me the wee dog." Before Sarina could warn her, Nana Orla reached in and picked up Wilma, tucking the dog close to her chest as she opened the door to the car.

"Be careful, Nana. Wilma bites," Justin warned, alarm wiping the smile from his face.

"I doubt that," Nana Orla responded, waving off the warning and placing a kiss on Wilma's little head. "Get out of the car and explain why you're the one bringing Adam's baby sister over instead of him? He's not been here for weeks and we have baby plans to make. And wedding plans, too. I don't want him to think he's getting away with not having a wedding."

Sarina got out of the car, squinting against the sunlight as she watched Justin fold the tiny woman into a hug, cutting it short when Wilma growled from her place tucked against Nana Orla's generous chest. Justin's grandmother was miniature, no more than five feet tall, her silver hair cut in a short angular bob that framed her face. Her eyes were a gray-blue and she wore little makeup except for the bright pink lipstick that matched the linen tunic and flowy pants she wore.

There was only a little physical resemblance between Justin and his Nana, but they had the same
energy and his grin was definitely due to her genetic
contribution. In fact, the more Sarina observed them
both together, the more she saw the similarity in
their smiles and the mischievous gleam in their eyes.

There might be two of her but Justin was the heir
apparent of her brand of trouble. Sarina smiled in
spite of herself, their obvious love and happiness at
seeing each other was infectious.

"Nana Orla, Adam asked me to bring Sarina over
here. I'm just helping out my best friend," Justin explained, sticking to the joint decision to let as few
people as possible know about the marriage.

Nana Orla's gaze ping-ponged between them
like she was at Wimbledon, her expression skeptical. "Don't give me the shite, Justin Ling. I saw the
two of you having some sort of altercation at the
baby gender reveal party and then the two of you
skittered off to Adam's office and you were in there
an awfully long time with Tess and Adam for me to
buy that crackpot explanation." She narrowed her
gaze, her eyes lighting up as she looked Sarina up
and down. "Are you pregnant, Sarina? Am I finally
going to get a great-grandchild?"

Sarina scooted backward, putting as much distance between her body and that insane idea as she
could. "Uh, no. I'm not pregnant."

"That's a shame," Nana Orla said.

"You already have five great-grandchildren, Nana Orla. You can drop the Princess Leia impression because I am not your only hope," Justin said, acting like there was nothing weird about this conversation. "I'm just helping out a friend. *We* are just helping out a friend."

Nana Orla considered him for a moment and then she swiveled, turning all of her intense focus on Sarina. "Are you going to live under my roof and tell me that pack of lies, too? Justin is used to sweet-talking everybody and getting away with it but I'm not so easily fooled. I watched him fine-tune those skills from the crib." She cocked her head to the side. "Spill it, Sarina. I know something's going on. What mess has my grandson dragged you into?"

Sarina glanced at Justin and he let out a long sigh. It was more resigned than frustrated so she took that as permission to come clean with Nana Orla...her new roomie.

"I'm his wife." Sarina rushed in to cut off the woman when she looked far too happy at this news. She didn't want to see the fallout of raising her hopes and then being the one to let her down but it couldn't be avoided. "Only temporarily. We're getting it annulled."

Nana Orla eyeballed Justin, her expression disapproving. "I'm guessing one of your trips to Vegas was involved." She shifted over and poked him in the chest. Her voice was chastising but her words were coated in the love and affection they clearly had flowing between them. Sarina looked away, pushing down the pang of longing that threatened to rise up in her chest. She turned back just in time to see Nana Orla flick him upside the head and then pat him on the cheek. "I've got you, Justin. I want to throttle you but I've got you."

"Geez. Warn a guy next time," Justin grumbled, rubbing the spot on the back of his head with exaggerated care.

The older lady shifted to include Sarina in her appraisal. Nana Orla scanned her up and down, her gaze assessing and thoroughly unnerving. It was like she could see right through her. "You look like a smart girl. How did you end up in this mess?"

Sarina ran through the events of that night, discarding all the things she was never going to tell someone's grandmother. She settled for the truth, minus a few details. "Justin is charming."

"He is," she said, nodding. "I just can't believe it worked on you."

"Hey!" Justin protested. "I'm right here."

Nana Orla waved him off. "I still love you anyway."

"Thank you, Nana Orla. One more thing. Don't tell my folks about the marriage."

She rolled her eyes, poking him one last time and wagging a finger of warning in his face. "Now you need me to lie for you, too? Jesus, Mary and Joseph.

I'm not doing this in the driveway, let's go inside and get Sarina settled."

Justin leaned in to kiss Nana Orla's cheek and Wilma bared her teeth, growls rumbling up from the little body cradled in his grandmother's arms.

"Well, at least Wilma's got sense to stay away from you and your 'charm.'"

Six

"How was the pajama party?" Justin asked.

He grinned over at Sarina in the passenger seat of his car, trying to gauge how she'd fared her first night with Nana Orla. His wife was a blank slate, her expression neutral as she gazed out the window as they cruised down the highway toward the Rise Up Center. She looked over at him, one eyebrow raised and a smirk tugging at her lips.

"Nana Orla stole my dog," she said, her tone telling him that she wasn't upset about this theft. "She bribed Wilma with lunch meat and tummy rubs so I slept alone."

Justin bit back the first thing that came to his lips: the offer to personally make sure she wasn't alone in the king-size bed in the guest suite of his nana's house. He had his own place, a sterile professionally decorated penthouse in the nicest retail/living town center in Silicon Valley. It was a place to sleep and grab a shower but he didn't consider it a home. He'd taken women there and ushered them out the next morning with a cup of coffee and an apology that he didn't have any food in the fridge. No, it wasn't a home and he didn't want to take Sarina there.

If he had a home, it was at Nana Orla's house. He'd crashed there before, usually when he just couldn't stomach so much family time with his parents in the main house. It was why he'd immediately thought of moving Sarina there; that house was a safe place, a place where a person could weather storms with support and love. Tough love—Nana Orla was always going to call you on your crap—but you never doubted you were loved.

"Don't worry, I'll make sure you get her back before you leave," he said, turning off the scenic highway, navigating busy streets and the typical glut of morning traffic. He glanced over at Sarina, surprised to find her still examining him. He maintained eye contact as long as he safely could, regretting that he hadn't ordered a driver today. Sarina intrigued him and he couldn't take his eyes off of her. "Although I'm not surprised Wilma gets along with Nana Orla."

"Me either," Sarina mused, her voice resigned but amused. "It kept her from asking too many questions so I'm not complaining." She laughed. "But I'm pretty sure that it was a reprieve, not a cease-fire, from the interrogation that is coming."

"You're probably right," he said, pausing before he asked a question he knew Sarina wasn't going to answer. "So, what don't you want to tell her?"

Sarina turned, her gaze locked on his face, and he could just feel the mind-your-own-business death ray aimed at him.

He shrugged. "What? I want to know more about my wife."

"You know what you need to know."

Justin knew he shouldn't poke at her but he couldn't stop himself. He wanted to know more about Sarina. If he was honest, he wanted to know everything. She fascinated him, and his desire for her had been immediate and visceral. He was a risk-taker, but that didn't include making foolish, drunken mistakes. His risks were calculated and thoughtful and while they looked reckless, they weren't stupid. Sarina had been...undeniable.

He pushed. Because he was Justin Ling. "Why'd you leave the army?"

She pushed back. Because she was Sarina Redhawk. "Why are you avoiding your parents?"

Okay, score a point for Team Redhawk. He hadn't said he was avoiding his parents but he'd shared the fact that he didn't fit into his family and he hadn't taken her to the mansion, he'd hidden her away at

Nana Orla's with strict instructions not to tell his folks.

She was right. But that didn't mean he was talking.

"You first," he said, winking at her.

The pause was longer than usual, no doubt giving him time to retract the question. She had read him wrong. He was fine with awkward silences. He could do this all day long.

"I had been in the army almost ten years and it was time for me to either sign up for the long haul toward retirement or to get out. The people I served with were all making the same decision, moving on with their families…it was time for me figure out my own path."

"And have you? Figured out your own path?"

She shook her head. "I answered. Your turn."

That was the deal. "My parents don't approve of my life choices. They think I could be better, could have done better. They think I don't act like a Ling."

Sarina turned fully in her seat, the expression on her face incredulous. "Wait. A billion-dollar company isn't good enough?"

Justin turned into the entrance to the center, pulling his car into one of the reserved spots at the front. He unfastened his seat belt and turned to face Sarina. "Look, I don't want to sound like a poor little rich kid, so don't take it that way." He paused, waiting until she nodded before he continued. Sarina's expression was placid, no indication of where she was falling on this. "I wasn't the high achiever like my brothers and sisters in the things that counted—school, grades, tests, appropriate behavior. I dropped out of Stanford after squeaking in because of my math ability, the one thing that made sense to me. I was dyslexic and a smart-ass and not the obedient son. They think my success is a fluke and that it will be gone in a minute." He mimicked his father's severe tone. *"It's not a stable undertaking."*

Sarina scoffed at that. "That's nuts. You're a mega success. Most parents would kill to have a son who's done as well as you have."

Justin shrugged it off. It wasn't what he hadn't thought a million times before. "My dad grew up in mainland China and broke all ties with his family, refusing an arranged marriage to be with my mom. They met when he was studying in England and she was there working at the university. They fell in love but his very traditional Chinese family disowned him when he ran off to the United States with her and got married. The marriage they were pushing on him had been a business arrangement and his refusal embarrassed them in the eyes of their friends and colleagues. Luckily my father had other family, also exiled, living here in California, and they took them in, helped him to build his business."

"So your parents were badass rebels who chose love. Sounds like they would totally embrace your way of life." She patted the dashboard of the expensive car they were sitting in. "And it looks like it worked out okay, at least from the monetary point of view."

"Yeah, yeah. But my parents went old-school when it came to raising their kids. They went super-traditional and conservative, in a way, to make up for their rebellion. They loved us, I never doubted that, but their expectations didn't leave room for a kid with a learning disability who had a gift for numbers and finance but who also likes to gamble and have no-string affairs with women." He shook his head, still stumped by his folks. "We were expected to do the private school to college to good job in a respected field of work that pays well and marriage with a suitable woman. My parents are the poster children for social status. If it involves doing the 'right' thing and supporting the 'right' charities and all that rot, they are on it. It would be funny if it wasn't so exhausting. It has put a strain on our relationship, to put it mildly."

Sarina considered this, nodding her head in understanding. "And your brothers and sisters went along with it?"

"Two doctors, a lawyer, and one taking over my dad's real estate business. I'm the black sheep."

Silence settled between them. Sarina looked at him, shrugging in answer. "I don't know what to say about that. Family is weird."

"It is." Justin didn't know what else to say about that, either. He'd just shared more with Sarina than he did with anyone and he needed to let it sit for a while. He needed to think about why it had been so easy to tell Sarina, why he'd *wanted* to tell Sarina. Time to change the subject. "This is the Rise Up Center."

He gestured at the building in front of them, opening his car door and motioning for Sarina to get out. He squinted against the bright sun. The sky was clear and the rising heat promised that today was going to be a scorcher. He clicked the lock on his key fob, joining his wife on the sidewalk. She was soaking it all in and he would be a liar to say that he wasn't a little bit proud of the admiration on her face.

"So, Nana Orla picked the name for the center. She's a *Hamilton* fan, so…we went with it."

"Like you were going to tell Nana Orla no."

"Yeah, that's never going to happen," he agreed with a grin. "This center is something that Adam and I thought up on one of our many all-nighters in college. We made a pledge that when we made a shit ton of money, we'd create a center for kids who were in the foster system, specifically targeting the older kids who have a smaller chance for adoption or who are close to aging out. This place is for those kids."

Sarina smiled, her face lit up with approval and interest. "This is amazing. You have *got* to show me around."

Justin grinned, opening the door and waving her inside. "That is exactly what I was hoping you'd say."

The center was incredible.

Sarina was completely blown away with what her brother and her husband had created. Taking over a large, abandoned community center and athletic facility in a poorer neighborhood, they'd gutted the building and created an indoor gymnasium, studios for dance and yoga classes, tutoring and group therapy rooms, and space for arts, crafts and music lessons. Outside they'd added all-new soccer fields, baseball diamond, tracks and a swimming pool. Kids from all over the Valley came here, using transportation provided by the center, and when they aged out, Rise Up provided a year of post support and classes geared toward helping them start their new life.

It was ridiculously amazing.

"Justin, this is incredible," Sarina said, grabbing his arm in her excitement. "I cannot believe what you're doing here. This is life-changing."

"That means a lot, coming from you." Justin shifted their bodies, grabbing her hand and weaving their fingers together. She wanted to touch him, needed to feel that connection, and she just went with it. It didn't make sense but nothing with Justin did. "We knew we wanted to do something good with the millions we'd make." He waggled his eyebrows, completely owning his cockiness. Considering that they'd made billions, it was well-deserved. She'd give him a pass. "We knew that we wanted to give back to the community. Adam always wondered about where you and Roan had ended up. He didn't know if it was in care or with a family. He worked with kids when we were in college, foster kids…this was his idea, really."

"And you just went along for the ride?" She knew that Justin's role was bigger than he let on. Everyone in the center, staff and kids alike, knew him by name and he knew personal details about them. It was clear that he spent a lot of time here. Not just writing checks or giving tours to big donors; nope, he was here all the time.

"Something like that," he said with a wink, leading her by the hand to the gymnasium where a dozen or so kids were playing basketball. She should have dropped his hand, broken the connection, but it felt good. It felt kind of right.

The group stopped the game and all turned when the doors clanged shut behind them. Within seconds their skeptical expressions morphed into wide grins and excited chatter erupted and bounced off the high ceilings.

"Justin!"

"Hey, man!"

The kids were ecstatic to see him, most of them swooping in to give him a hug or a back slap. He had a connection with these kids. He loved them and they loved him right back. She was starting to think that resisting the charisma of Justin Ling was easier said than done.

Justin turned and led her over, still holding her hand as he introduced his fan club. "That's Mike, Sarah, Ruben, Marcus, Big Pete, Little Pete, Katie, Teresa and Jose."

Each kid saluted her in turn, their smiles genuine even if a little shy. All of their gazes drifted down to where her hand joined with Justin's. She didn't miss the looks they gave each other. Sarina let go of Justin before anyone got the wrong idea, extending it to shake each of their hands.

"I'm Sarina Redhawk. Nice to meet you."

The impact of her name was immediate. Their grins got even wider, their excitement almost palpable.

"What? You're Adam's sister?"

"That is so cool."

"Does Adam know you're hitting on his sister, man?" The last question came from Little Pete, a tall kid who reached to at least six and half feet. Big Pete was closer to seven feet, so the name was appropriate. "He's gonna kill you."

"Adam knows, you goofball." Justin lightly punched the boy in the arm. "And he doesn't scare me."

"Uh-huh," Little Pete mused, his expression saying that he didn't believe any of it. He tossed the basketball at Justin, who caught it easily. "You got time for a game?"

Justin tossed the ball back, shaking his head. "No man, I've got to get back to the office. We're working a big deal but I'll come back in a couple of days, I promise."

"I can stay." Sarina didn't realize she'd said it until everyone turned to face her. She twisted to look at Justin. "I've got nowhere to be and this is where I'm going to be working for the next few weeks. Why not start now?" She reached over and popped the ball out of Little Pete's hand, dribbling past him to make the shot. The ball swooshed through the net and all the kids whooped and hollered. "I'm a little rusty but I think I can remember how to play."

"All right," Katie said, throwing an exaggerated wave at Justin, motioning for him to exit the gym. "You can go. We've got Sarina."

Justin grabbed his chest in mock dismay, stumbling back from the group. "Whoa, you guys suck."

The kids erupted in laughter, piling on Justin to offer him hugs of apology.

"Okay, okay." Justin held his hands up in surrender. "I'd love to leave Sarina here but I'm her ride, guys. She's got to go."

"I can get a ride back to the house," Sarina said. It couldn't be that hard to order an Uber or to get Adam to come get her. "I'm a grown person. If I could figure out how to get around Afghanistan, I can get home."

"You were over there?" Katie asked, her voice a little awestruck.

Sarina grinned at her. "Yeah. Two tours." She looked around at the group of kids. They would be spending a lot of time together the next few weeks. If they were going to trust her, she needed to let them know she trusted them. "I joined the army when I aged out of care."

"So, you weren't adopted like Adam?" This time the question came from Marcus. He was shy, speaking out from behind Mike's back, but his smile was genuine if tentative.

"I was…" She faltered at this part. Her past was complicated and hadn't been pleasant to live through, and talking about it wasn't easy, either. Justin was watching her, his eyes inquisitive but his expression kind. He inclined his head, letting her know that it was up to her. She took a breath and dived in. "I was adopted but it didn't work out."

"They gave you back?" Teresa was disgusted, her hand on her hip in indication.

"No. CPS came in, took me out and put me back in the system." She debated about how to tell the next part, going for a middle-of-the-road answer. "My adoptive parents weren't great people and they didn't treat me so well. Care wasn't great but was better than what I had."

Silence fell on the group and she watched as each of the kids processed her story.

"That really sucks, Sarina," Marcus said, nodding along with the other kids. "It's a good thing that you're here. You've been in the system so that makes you a center kid. You belong here with us."

And just like that, she was one of them. It felt good. Right. As easy as it was with Justin.

Sarina nodded at each of them in thanks, letting a grin take over her face. It was time to lift the mood in this joint. "Well, then it won't hurt so much when I kick all of your butts."

Catcalls and trash talk filled the room as the kids moved into their positions on the court. Justin came up beside her, one arm looping around her waist as he drew her in closer. He was warm, body as firm and taut as she remembered, and he still smelled so damn good. Sarina leaned into him involuntarily, giving in to the pull of attraction that always pulsed between them.

"You're pretty amazing, Sarina Redhawk Ling," he murmured low so that only she could hear. She ignored the little flip her heart did when she heard her name joined with his. "It took me months to get these kids to accept me like that."

"Well, I'm a center kid. You heard Marcus." Sarina was more pleased with the approval in Justin's eyes and voice than she wanted to admit. Knowing that he didn't pity her or pepper her with a million questions meant a lot. He was giving her the time and space she needed to share, or not. It was seductive.

And she didn't mind the use of her married name. Not at all.

That was…interesting.

Justin gauged her mood accurately and let it drop. Instead he pulled out his key fob and dangled it in front of her. "I'll call a car to come get me and take me to the office. I'll leave the Porsche for you."

"What? You're going to leave me your one-hundred-thousand-dollar sports car? Are you high?"

"California is a community property state so technically, the car is half yours," Justin answered, jangling the key fob so that it made a metallic clinking sound. His grin slid into seductive, a little dirty. "Come on, you know you want to drive it. If I recall, you prefer a wild ride."

Sarina flushed, her skin hot and goose bumps racing down her arms. She remembered this Justin.

This Justin had kept her up all night.

She let her gaze drift down to his mouth, her heart racing when his lips curved into a smile that told her he knew exactly where her thoughts had gone. He leaned in, so close she almost tasted his kiss.

"Are we going to play ball or are you two going to kiss it out?"

Sarina had no idea which kid said it but it broke the tension immediately. Justin's grin got wider and he rolled his eyes, releasing her from his hold.

Sarina snatched the key fob out of Justin's hand, her grin wide and her heart light for the first time in a long time. "Get out of here. I'm going to play some ball."

Seven

"Your car handles like a dream, Justin."

Sarina stretched out her hand, dangling the key fob over the open palm of the car's owner. Justin was kicked back on a lounge chair by the pool at Nana Orla's house, his grin as warm as the lingering sunshine. The beer in his other hand looked as cool as the water spilling out of the fountain water feature. At the last minute she yanked back her hand.

"Nope." She smiled at his shocked expression. "No beer, no expensive car keys."

"Are you holding my car hostage until I get you a beer?"

Sarina glanced over at Nana Orla, winking at the older woman. "He's cute *and* smart. If *only* he was rich."

Nana Orla cracked up, a belly laugh that had her doubled over on her lounger. "Justin, if you let this girl go I will disown you."

"*Really*, Nana? I thought I was your favorite!" Justin said, fishing an ice-cold bottle out of the outdoor fridge, popping it open and heading back over to Sarina.

"I don't have any favorites, Justin. I love all of my grandkids equally," Nana Orla assured him. "But if you don't keep this girl, you won't be my favorite anymore."

"You wound me, Nana. I'm gutted." Justin handed the beer to Sarina.

She took it and slid into his vacant lounger with a grin on her face, effectively stealing his seat. "Sorry. You're too slow."

Justin paused, his head cocked at her, his smile big but confused. "What's gotten into you?" He held his hands up in the universal gesture for surrender. "Don't get me wrong. This is the Sarina I met in Vegas and I like her a lot. I'm just wondering where the grumpy, prickly one went and is she coming back?"

Nana Orla snorted. "If that's your best pickup line it's no wonder you're single."

"Ignore him." Sarina waved him off. She was riding high and nothing was going to knock her off this mountain. "I had a great day with the kids at the center. They're so smart and brave and the center is extraordinary. I think I can do some good with them in the next few weeks. You and Adam have created something really special there."

Justin sat down, straddling the lounger to face her. He reached out to take her hand and she let him, leaning into the moment. His smile was bright and contagious and only for her.

"You had a good day, yeah?" Justin asked, his thumb rubbing softly against her wrist. It was mesmerizing, sucking her into his orbit once again. She knew it was a bad idea but she couldn't bring herself to stop it.

"Yeah, I did." She leaned forward; it was impossible to wipe the smile off her face. "Those kids are so great. Thank you for taking me there."

"I knew you'd love it."

"Oh, Ma, I didn't know you had company."

Sarina jumped at the female, Irish-tinged voice, shifting quickly to look over her shoulder at the couple standing on the patio. Justin stilled beside her, his fingers tightening on her own, his body tense. The couple were in their early 60s, tan and fit and dressed for a cocktail event in clothes that reeked of money and status. They were both tall, the man broad-shouldered with dark hair sprinkled heavily with silver. The woman was also willowy, but athletic and fit, with dark hair pulled up into a sleek updo. But what stood out to Sarina most was the fact that the woman had Justin's smile and the man moved like him, quick but controlled and smooth.

It didn't take a genius to figure out that they were Justin's parents, Mr. and Mrs. Ling.

It also didn't take a Mensa member to realize that they were not thrilled that she was sitting here holding their son's hand.

Nana Orla put her drink down on the little side table before rising from her lounger and greeting the newcomers with open arms.

"Come here, you two. Give someone a heart attack sneaking up on somebody like that." She pulled them both in, fussing over them as she kept talking. "Where are you going all dressed up? It's Wednesday. What could possibly be happening on a Wednesday?"

"It's a cocktail party to meet the new director of the arts coalition, Mother. I thought I told you," Saoirse Ling responded, her gaze settled intently on Sarina, so focused it was almost like a physical touch. "Who is your guest, Ma?"

Her accent wasn't as intense as Nana Orla's, softened by either years spent in the United States or purposefully polished down to the point where it hinted at time spent abroad in places more glamorous than California. But her gaze was 100 percent her mother's, inquisitive and not missing a thing.

Justin's father was just as intense but more quiet and removed. Sarina got the impression that he didn't have much to say but that he missed nothing, especially where his children were concerned.

Either way Sarina had met them before; they were echoes of the countless parents of potential friends she'd met through the years who'd been thrilled that little Molly/Susie/Amanda had a new buddy until they'd realized it was a kid in foster care. Especially a kid in foster care who had a folder of failures and problems as she moved from home to home. She couldn't blame them for protecting their kids, but she couldn't forgive them, either.

Mr. and Mrs. Ling weren't thrilled at the stray Justin had brought home this time if their reactions were any indicator. She allowed herself a small huff of laughter when she thought about how they'd react if they knew she was their daughter in-law.

"My new friend is Sarina Redhawk," Nana Orla answered, turning to grin down at her, letting everyone know that she was very welcome here. It was a kind gesture, protective, and it set Sarina on alert. "She's staying with me for a few weeks while she assists Justin at the Rise Up Center." Nana Orla gestured to the newcomers. "You've probably guessed that these are Justin's parents, Allan and Saoirse."

"Redhawk?" Allan Ling, looking at her more closely. Man, his razor-sharp, dark-eyed gaze reminded her so much of Justin. "Adam's sister? The one who recently left the army?"

Sarina stood, noting that Justin rose with her and

let go of her hand but kept a protective hand at her back. She held out her hand, falling back on her military training to handle this awkward situation. "Yes, sir. It's nice to meet you."

He took her hand, shaking it and nodding in greeting. "Thank you for your service, Sarina. Adam speaks highly of you."

"I think Adam is a good brother, sir." She shot a glance at Nana Orla. "I'm grateful to Nana Orla for letting me stay here while I have my motorcycle fixed. She's a wonderful lady."

"Yes, well, Ma can't resist a stray in need." Saoirse interjected, her smile an attempt to dull the edges of her blade. She didn't want to kill, only wound and warn. Sarina appreciated the transparency in the rules of engagement. "Justin gets that from her."

"Well, if that's true, then they've found the right project in the Rise Up Center," Sarina replied, taking pains to keep her words and tone respectful, but making sure her position was clear. She didn't want to make trouble for Justin or Nana Orla but she wasn't going to let anyone put down their incredible hearts. "They are doing incredible things with those kids… I guess you'd call them 'strays.'"

Justin's hand on her back slid around her waist, drawing her ever so slightly closer to him. It wasn't a big move but it made his point and both of his parents noticed. Both tensed, standing taller and straighter in their fancy clothes.

"Mom and Dad, Sarina has agreed to fill in at the center for the next few weeks while we look for a new director." He looked at her, his gaze full of admiration and his smile only for her. "We are lucky to have her. She's already bonded with some of the kids."

There was a long pause but nobody rushed to fill it. *Awkward* was the appropriate word but it didn't even come close to describing the width and breadth of all the things unsaid. Mrs. Ling finally broke the impasse and it was like someone had let the air out of an explosive-filled balloon.

"Well, that's nice, although it will be a shame when you have to go. But we all understand, and appreciate your work for these few weeks." She reached out to give a half hug to her mother as they prepared to leave. Then she let the other shoe drop so casually that it almost didn't make an impact. "Justin, Heather Scarborough will be at this party. I'll make sure to tell her you said hello."

Justin cleared his throat. "Sure, Mom. Tell her I said hello."

Sarina didn't have to be a genius to read between the lines here. Saoirse didn't like whatever she sensed was going on between her and Justin and she made sure that Sarina knew that her presence in his life had a shelf life. *Check*. She was also reminded that Justin had other options, more suitable options who attended Wednesday-night charity parties and got along with his mother. *Check*. Message received.

They watched as the Lings made their exit, heading toward their Mercedes and leaving behind a lingering scent of expensive perfume, aftershave and money. They had killed the mood for the evening, ushering in a chill that mimicked the one brought on by the setting of the sun.

Justin let out a heavy sigh, his hand tightening on her waist as he looked into her eyes. "Well, you met your in-laws."

It wasn't funny but it let loose the tension in her shoulders, stress from the last few moments expelled in a laugh that sounded off to her ears. Holy hell, why was a short-term marriage suddenly so complicated? It didn't take a rocket scientist to figure that out. It was complicated because she cared for Justin and so it mattered that his parents thought she was trash.

And if she was honest, they were just the latest in the long line of parents who didn't think she was good enough for their kids, their lives. Some things never changed.

She couldn't stop how she felt. But she could stop her feelings for Justin from growing any bigger.

Sarina moved to go inside. She'd take a shower, grab something to eat and hide in her room watching Netflix. She needed time to process, to construct stronger barriers around her feelings when it came to Justin Ling. She needed to remember that they did have a shelf life, that there was a pending divorce looming between them.

"Sarina, come with me. I want to show you something."

It was his voice. Soft, intimate, a tone and cadence she knew was one he only used with her. All he had to do was say her name and all her reservations vanished. She'd waited her whole life to have someone look at her the way he did, speak to her the way he did.

Even if it was just for now, she couldn't walk away from it.

Justin took her hand and scooped up two beers, saying a quick goodbye to Nana Orla. He led her across the lawn toward the grove of trees filling the space between the house and rising hills. It was quiet and serene here, a million miles away from the bustle of the Silicon Valley just beyond the perimeter of the property. Here, it was just the two of them; no parents, no long-lost brothers, no lawyers or investors.

They entered the copse of trees, the waning sunlight now just dapples of light on the ground all around them. It was like nature's version of those fairy lights people draped all over the place at the holidays. The temperature dropped in the shade of the trees, causing goosebumps to erupt on her skin. Or it could have just been anticipation that had her alert and aware of every breath and brush of skin as they walked side by side.

It took her a moment to adjust to the shadows and then she saw it. A small house, nestled in the crook of the limbs of a huge old tree. It was made of wood, so expertly interwoven with the trees around it that it looked like it had been there forever. A staircase curved along the tree trunk, and led to the structure now rising up directly over their heads.

Justin flashed her a smile that took over his face, lighting his eyes up with childish delight. She smiled back, unable to resist his undiluted joy or the tug of his hand as he led her up the stairs.

If she thought the approach was amazing, the inside of the structure took her breath away. Exposed hardwood, maybe oak or pecan, formed the one-room tree house, the ceiling tall enough for them to stand easily, glass skylights and a wall of windows giving them a full view of their surroundings and the sky. From this vantage point, everything disappeared except for the treetops and the stars filling up the darkening sky.

"Oh my God," Sarina breathed out, her eyes darting from one detail to the next. Shelves built into the walls held books, candles, a fallen bird's nest, the mementos of exploration and indulgence. Colorful quilts were piled on an oversize daybed stationed in the middle of the room, an inviting place to take a nap, read a book or gaze at the stars.

Justin let go of her hand, placing the bottles on the small table next to the daybed before walking over to the windows and unlatching them in several places before he pushed them to the side, effectively joining this space with the great outdoors.

"Justin, I have never seen anything like this in my life."

"It's awesome, isn't it?" His smile was now full of pride; he was clearly pleased that she liked his show-and-tell surprise. It made her blood warm, knowing that her opinion mattered so much to him. "Nana Orla didn't want us to forget what it was like to just be kids, so she had this built for us when I was little. It was just a simple tree fort back then but I had it reno-vated a couple of years ago, had an architect shore up the structure, add the windows and electricity that can run a small fridge and add a powder room at the back. It's one of my favorite places in the world."

"This is incredible. I cannot believe it. It's like something in a fairy tale."

Justin's grin got wider as he opened the two bot-tles, settling down on the daybed and stretching his long legs out in front of him. He nodded toward the spot next to him. "Sit down. Check out the stars."

She knew that this was dangerous territory. This man, the stars, a tree house. Everything was tailor-made for her to do something foolish. She did it anyway.

The bed was comfortable, perfectly situated to give them the best view of the stars that were tak-ing over the darkening sky. The birds were settling down for the night, adding their own muted sounds to the show.

Justin's arm stretched out on the daybed behind her, his movement shifting the cushions between them and easing their bodies together so that they touched from shoulder to knee, their body warmth mingling and causing Sarina to shiver with the contrast of the cooler night air.

"You know what was the worst thing about waking up in Vegas and realizing you were gone?" Justin asked, his voice low, as if he thought he'd spook her.

She shook her head. She had her suspicions, but really she didn't know. She only knew how she'd felt when she'd realized that she had to leave.

"It wasn't that I was horrified or embarrassed about waking up married. It was the thought that I'd made up the way we connected, the way I felt when I was with you." He swallowed hard, taking a sip from his beer before continuing. "I wanted that to be as real as I thought it was. I still do, even if I know we can't stay together."

She could go two ways with this: she could lie and tell him that it was just the shots at the bar, or she could tell him the truth and assure him that she'd felt it, too. But she knew she couldn't lie because she understood completely what he was saying, because it was the reason she'd left.

"It was real, Justin," she whispered, taking a deep breath to steady the frantic beat of her heart. "It was why I had to leave."

Justin placed his beer bottle on the table and turned to her, his free hand sliding over her jaw, fingers winding into her hair. She lifted her face to his, shutting her eyes to the intensity of his gaze at the same time his mouth pressed against her own. Soft lips, quick breaths, and then groans and mouths opening to each other, tongues tangling and the kiss deepening to the point where she didn't know where she ended and he began.

Sarina wrapped her arms around his neck, hungry to be as close to him as she could get, her body craving what it remembered was so good. Justin's hands roamed over her body, coasting over her back, her hip, back into her hair. Everywhere he touched her was liquid heat, nerve endings responding to him and sending messages to her brain that defied logic and drove out any rational thought.

It was need and connection and pheromones and hunger.

Justin groaned, lifting her onto his lap. She straddled him, the tender, aroused center of her body pressed against his hard dick under his jeans. Sarina gasped, releasing his mouth as she threw her head back, eyes open, with nothing but the stars above and Justin's hard, sexy body beneath.

"Damn, Sarina," Justin moaned out beneath her as his body bucked up to meet every one of her downward thrusts. His fingers went to the neckline of her V-neck T-shirt, tugging it and the soft cup of her bra down to expose a nipple. She looked down just in time to see his mouth close over the tight peak and then she felt the tug of his wet, hot mouth on her nipple. She was close, so close.

It was so primal, something she hadn't indulged in since a teenager, the not-so-innocent humping of two bodies together as they pursued one of life's best gifts. But she couldn't get naked with Justin, not now. It was too much. Her body wanted him but she couldn't be that vulnerable. Not when she knew she had to leave.

But she would be selfish and take what she could. Because she needed him.

She bore down on his hard length, pleased when he released her breast on a moan that was half pain and half pleasure. Their eyes locked, mouths swollen and lips wet as they ground their bodies together, both needing the same thing.

One minute she was on the edge and the next she was arching into him, crying out loudly as her orgasm hit her like a bolt of lightning. Hot, intense, sharp-edged with pleasure that tightened every muscle in her body, it was drawn out by the sound of Justin moaning underneath her, his hips and cock pulsing against her body as he came.

Sarina collapsed against him, trying to catch her breath and glad for his arms around her as she tried to wrap her brain around what had just happened.

It had been real in Vegas. It was real in the here and now.

But it didn't change anything.

Eight

Sarina was avoiding him.

The mind-blowing orgasm in the tree house had been unbelievably hot. They'd needed to talk about it but in true Justin and Sarina avoidance protocol, they'd cleaned themselves up, headed back to the house and then retreated to their corners to process what had just happened.

And two days had gone by with no contact and it was driving him nuts.

He'd gone to the office, burying himself in the financials he was working up to accompany the deal they were executing with the investors at Aerospace Link. This wasn't a typical deal for Redhawk/Ling but it was exciting. In the past, they'd been the ones seeking people to assist them, doing the work to prove that they were a good investment. Now they were one of the frontrunners in app and cloud-based technology and Aerospace Link was a leader in satellites. And this new venture would put them both in the position of leading the next wave of technological innovation.

This was a collaboration that would lead to opportunities that Redhawk/Ling wanted and needed to be a part of in order to solidify their lead in the market, so nothing could jeopardize it. They had made the money and the money had gotten them a spot at the table but Justin and Adam wanted to be at the head of the table and this deal would put them there. Which was why it was so important to keep the marriage to Sarina a secret.

Adam wasn't wrong when he said that Justin's reputation wasn't always an asset to the company. People admired his ability to crunch numbers and project trends in finance, to think outside of the box and make people a shit ton of money. There was a reason why the upstart companies who had nothing to lose were the ones that shook things up and pushed the boundaries. Once people got rich they got scared and they played it safe.

So they didn't like that he loved poker, high-stakes poker with players who could match his skill. Outsiders saw his participation as an indication that he lacked control and that he had a problem. But he wasn't an addict, he was a puzzle solver, a human calculator. It wasn't risky, it was statistics and probabilities. Poker was numbers and numbers always made sense to Justin; it wasn't risky for him because it was just math.

But the only thing that they mistrusted more than the poker was the women. No matter how trendsetting the men and women of Silicon Valley were supposed to be they were pure 1950s when it came to sex. Stability was going home to the same partner every night for dinner, and investors preferred to trust people who were *stable* with their bank accounts.

Justin was never going to apologize for enjoying sex with a variety of partners. His parents would love for him to settle down but the women he picked weren't there for *him*. They showed up for his money and they stayed for the orgasms and the good times. Everybody was an adult and everybody knew the rules. Nobody got attached and nobody got hurt.

But Sarina was different. He wasn't in love with her but they had *something*. A connection. She made him feel good, like he was doing it right by doing it his way.

Which is why he was walking into the Rise Up Center in the middle of the day to see her when he should have been at the office. Estelle, the assistant extraordinaire he shared with Adam, had given him a sly smile and amused side-eye when he'd told her that he'd be taking the rest of the day. He didn't even stop to wonder how she knew what he was up to; Estelle knew everything.

After a quick exchange with Kori at the center's front desk, he headed to the rock climbing room, following the excited voices.

He entered the space, familiar to him since he'd designed it. He'd wanted it to be a place for the kids to push themselves, to try something new and different. The result was a room surrounded by climbing walls from floor to ceiling with every level from beginner to advanced. The kids loved it.

The sight of it made him a little queasy.

Teresa spotted him first, hanging from a rope halfway up the wall. "Hey, Justin! You here to join us? Get your climb on?"

"Holy crap, Teresa, pay attention to what you're doing!" Justin shouted, his unease impossible to hide. Didn't she see how far up she was? And with nothing beneath her but air. He shuddered a little.

"Green ain't your color, man!" Big Pete joked, inspecting his equipment on one of the benches that ran along the center of the room.

Justin waved them off, eyes searching for the person he came here to see. He scanned the room, heart jumping in his chest when he spotted a familiar figure, wearing black form-fitting clothes and hovering forty feet above the ground. Sarina was stunning, her body strong and in perfect control as she strained to climb higher, muscles tense with the effort.

His fingers flexed, memories of touching her body, gliding along her smooth skin as she responded so sweetly to the passion that flared between the two of them. The other evening in the tree house it had been combustible, something he'd known was coming and he'd done nothing to stop. The next few weeks were going to be agony if he stayed around her and couldn't touch her.

But he knew that staying away was going to be impossible.

His current location was proof of that.

He held his breath as she reached the top, grinning down at the kids who yelled out their congratulations to her. Their eyes locked and it was a moment of recognition, a spark, and he saw delight in her gaze. It made his stomach flip and he grinned up at her unabashedly, not caring who saw. His excitement didn't even dim when she checked her equipment, glanced behind her and then descended at a rate of speed that made the floor move under his feet.

Damn it. Why had he built this rock climbing gym?

Sarina landed with sure-footed confidence, turning to high-five the kids who swarmed around her to offer their congratulations. She laughed, her usual placid expression replaced with the enthusiastic affection she already had for the kids. He gave himself an inner high five for taking the chance that she would be the right fit for this group. They were older kids, pasts full of disappointment and with few adults to look up to, but he'd known that they'd find what they needed in Sarina.

"Don't you have a job?" Sarina's question broke into his thoughts. She walked over to him, hand on her hip and head cocked to the side. "Don't you have a bunch of tech billionaire things to do?"

He laughed, moving in closer just to catch a little bit of the citrus scent that clung to her hair and skin. His first impulse was to lean in and kiss her but he knew they had an audience. A young, impressionable audience.

An audience that would rat them out to Adam.

"I do, but I wanted to invite myself over tonight. I've got a present."

"For me?" she asked, her nose scrunched up in confusion. "For what?"

He shook his head, knowing she'd never accept a gift from him. "No way. It's for Wilma."

"Ah," she replied, giving him a dubious side-eye. "You know that she can't be bribed."

"A man has to try."

"Good luck with that." Sarina unhooked the equipment from around her waist, offering it up to him. "You want to climb?"

He couldn't back up fast enough. "Oh no."

"He's afraid of heights, Sarina," Katie offered. "We can't get him up there for love or money."

"Really?" Sarina looked really confused now. "What about the tree house? You know it's up in the air, right? Off the ground?"

"Yeah, but it has a floor. I'm okay with things that have floors. I just can't have the vast expanse of nothing below me."

Sarina moved into him, her fingers brushing against his midriff. She meant it to be teasing, comforting, but it made him ache for her. "So I guess you wouldn't walk the Grand Canyon Skywalk with me?"

He reached down and took her hand, his thumb rubbing over her knuckles. "Not if it doesn't have a floor."

"Oh no. It's a glass bridge that extends seventy feet out beyond the rim of the Grand Canyon and four thousand feet above the bottom of the canyon. My old master sergeant said that if you stand on it you can look down and see your future."

"Is that before or after you puke?" he asked, horrified by the image that popped into his mind.

"Ha! Before, I would guess." Sarina winked at him, turning and pointing at Marcus. "You ready?"

The boy nodded, his expression tentative as he shifted his big eyes between Sarina and the wall.

"Don't worry. We'll do this together," she assured him, giving his arm a squeeze of encouragement.

Justin moved back, keeping his eye focused on his

wife and the young man she gently guided through the steps of preparing to climb. Marcus was nervous but Sarina was calm, telling him that he could do it and running him the through the steps until he could repeat it back to her verbatim.

They positioned themselves along the wall, both making the final preparation to ascend. Sarina looked around at the kids standing around. "Come on, join us. Marcus needs the support and he's *sidanelv*—that's Cherokee for *family*. We don't let our family do it alone, right?"

Big Pete, Katie and Teresa all stepped up and prepared to climb with their friend. And they did it—together. Marcus stumbled at times and he was scared, but the other kids and Sarina kept him going, cheering him on and giving him helpful pointers when necessary. Forty-five minutes later Marcus was standing on the ground again, smiling proudly as his buddies all piled on with hugs and high fives.

Hair mussed and cheeks pink with her efforts, her grin contagious, Sarina moved over to Justin. "So, when am I going to get you up on that wall?"

"I think you need to reconcile yourself to disappointment," Justin said, helping her as she divested herself of her equipment again. He sneaked a peek at her, turning over in his head something he'd wondered about since meeting Sarina. "You were really good with him. I could see your military training working so well and it makes me wonder why you left the army when you were obviously made for it."

Sarina messed with the stuff in her hands, taking so long that he wasn't sure she was going to answer him. When she did, it was in a quiet tone, edged with regret and little wistfulness. "The army works because we all have the same purpose but also because we become a family for one another. My people had moved on to the next duty station, left the service, gotten married and had babies. It was time for me to find my own life, my own future."

Justin debated asking her the question on his mind. The obvious question. He did it anyway. He wasn't good with waiting. "How is that working out for you?"

She flashed him a half smile, shaking her hair out of her eyes. "I'm working on it."

And while he knew he shouldn't, he wanted her plans to include him.

Nine

"Permission to come aboard?"

Sarina popped her head out the window of the tree house and looked down at the man standing at the bottom of the steps. Justin was so sexy, wearing a black T-shirt and shorts, a pair of flip-flops on his long feet. He had his sunglasses pushed up on top of his head and he was holding a bag with a local sandwich shop name on the side in one hand and a six-pack of beer in the other.

It had only been a couple of hours since she'd seen him at the center and he was still hot. Still making her stomach flip with the jolt of heated sensual recognition.

"Justin, that's for boats, not tree houses," she chastised him with a laugh. "And this is *your* tree house."

"Nope. I think I've lost ownership of the tree house while you and Wilma are in residence. That's what Nana Orla says," he answered, nodding toward his uplifted hands. "I come bearing food and drink."

"Well, in that case, come on up."

Sarina retreated into the tree house, pulling the scrunchie off her hair and fluffing it up. She caught her reflection in the small mirror over the bookcase on the wall; her cheeks were flushed even without a stitch of makeup. She'd seen the photos online of Justin with women and they were all beauty queens with perfect hair, clothes and makeup. Sarina had never worried about it before and now was too late with her messy hair and old cotton sundress.

She couldn't do anything about it in the next five seconds She was who she was.

And why was she thinking about this at all? This was never going to be anything. Her husband wouldn't be her husband in a few short weeks. She needed to stop acting like every encounter with him was a first date. It wasn't anything like that.

So why did it feel like that's exactly what it was?

"You look gorgeous."

Sarina spun, surprised to see Justin standing behind her so soon. He must have raced up the steps and here he was, his expression telling her that he liked what he saw. She blushed, heat spreading over her skin like the breeze whispering through the windows of the tree house.

Wilma growled from her little nest of blankets on the daybed. She was buried underneath the covers; the only visible part of her little body was her nose and two big dark eyes.

"Oh wait, I forgot to offer my tribute to the lady of the manor," Justin said, dumping the food and the beer on the side table. He fished a little gift bag covered in a design of various cartoon dogs out of his pocket, the paper crumpled from being shoved in there. "I noticed that our grumpy Wilma needed a new collar and tag. I took the liberty of getting her one that's fit for the badass she is."

Sarina took the bag from him, opened it and pulled out the little collar. It was black leather with three rows of shiny silver studs and a metal piece that had "Wilma" engraved on it. From it dangled a motorcycle-shaped silver tag with Sarina's name and cell phone number. It was perfect.

"I figured she'd love the motorcycle babe theme. You know, for when you get your bike back and you two start your road trip up all over again." Justin dipped his head, his demeanor unsure and shy.

"I love it. She'll love it." Sarina wavered, not sure of what she should do and finally sitting down next to Wilma, drawing the little dog onto her lap. She removed the old collar, easing the new one around her neck and fastening it securely. It looked great on her. "She looks like a little badass."

"She does."

"Thank you, Justin," Sarina said, nodding her head when Justin reached out to pet the dog's head. Wilma growled at first, dipping her head in submission when Justin stroked the silky spot between her ears. She hid her face in the crook of Sarina's arm, peeking out to look up at Justin with sweet, sad eyes. "Wilma says thank you, too."

"She didn't bite me. I'll take that as a win."

Sarina put down the little dog and they both watched as she crossed the room, curling up in a ball on a floor cushion. Wilma burrowed into the fabric, huffing out a long sigh before she closed her eyes and ignored the humans.

"Here, I'll thank you properly," Sarina said, rising to her feet and pulling Justin to her in a soft, sweet kiss. Just barely a brush of the lips; she meant it to be brief, a throwaway, but she felt it down to her toes.

His arms slid around her waist and she gripped them, drawing him closer to her body. They didn't deepen the kiss; it was enough to be wrapped around each other, sinking into the sweetness of the moment.

"Sarina," Justin breathed, his fingertips ghosting over her face, tracing her lips and cheekbones. "I want you all the time."

"I want you, too," she sighed, kissing his palm,

her breath catching in her chest. "This is such a bad idea."

"The worst," he agreed, tightening his hold when she tried to pull away. "The best." He groaned, kissing her mouth, his tongue dipping inside, teasing her. Driving her crazy. "I think we should keep doing it."

"Of course you do." Sarina smiled against his lips. She should be putting an end to this but she just couldn't. It was beyond her power. "You *are* a gambler, right?"

"Hear me out," Justin said, pulling back enough to look her in the eye. "We have this connection, attraction, that has been there from the first. But neither of us is looking for anything serious or permanent, right?"

"If we were, we'd stay married."

"Exactly." Justin ran his thumb across her bottom lip, visibly holding back a moan when she licked it. "But I'm here and you're here for the next few weeks. We want each other. We know we're good together. So why not indulge? All we're going to do is give in over and over and then beat ourselves up for it." He pulled her closer and she could feel the heat of him, the hardness of his cock pressed against her body. "I want to be inside you again. I want to make you fall apart all over me. That's what I want, Sarina."

Sarina considered him; there were a million reasons why she should say no to this and push him away. She wasn't classy enough to fit in his life. She didn't know how to be with someone in a relationship. They weren't headed for a happily ever after. Their divorce papers were in the works.

But the bottom line was that she didn't want to. She was lonely, or at least tired of being alone in her bed, and she knew that Justin wouldn't try to stop her when it was time for her to leave.

And she wanted him. She liked the way he looked at her, as if she was important to him, as if she had a power over him that she'd never had with anyone else. The power to linger, to be remembered, to be yearned for.

But she'd never tell him that. It wasn't necessary for their current arrangement.

"Yes. I want you inside me again. Please, Justin."

"Thank God," he breathed and she was suddenly surrounded by him. His hard, muscled arms wrapped around her and his mouth possessed hers. The kiss was intense, hungry, and so was his touch as it roamed all over her body, tracing heat over her bare skin.

She clutched at him, finding it frustrating to be unable to get close enough. To feel enough. Sarina tugged him back, sitting down on the mattress of the daybed and pulling him down on top of her. She needed to feel his weight on her, to have something to strain against, something to hold on to when he drove her out of her mind.

"Justin, please." She reached down, snagging the

hem of his T-shirt and dragging it over his head. Sarina sighed, some of the tension in her gut easing when she touched him, skimmed her fingertips over the warm expanse of his skin. It was as if her body had been waiting for this moment, the moment when she could feel him again, connect with him again. "I remember this."

Sarina traced a finger down his chest, over the tensing muscles of his abdomen to the edge of his waistband. She watched his face, the way he bit his lip in pleasure, the soft flutter of his eyelashes as he fought the urge to close his eyes and just sink into the anticipation of her touch.

"Do you remember this?" she asked as she unfastened the button on his shorts and eased down the zipper. His cock was hard, straining upward behind his boxer briefs, and she wasted no time in easing down the fabric and holding him, hot and heavy in her hand.

"Damn, Sarina. Touch me, please." Justin panted above her, his words deep and guttural.

She was never going to tell him no, never going to deny him. Not this. Not when she wanted to taste him again so very badly.

Sarina shoved him over onto his back, using the movement to push down his shorts and boxer briefs to his thighs and then slide them down his legs. Justin sprawled out beneath her, his long, hard body so gorgeous in the sunlight that filtered through the windows of the tree house.

"You don't have to," he whispered, his fingers tangled in her hair.

"But I want to. I need to taste you."

Sarina leaned over and took him in her mouth, tentatively at first as she got used to the width and length of him. He smelled of heat and salt and sweat and the sand-and-sun fragrance that was Justin to her. He reached down and wrapped his long fingers around his dick as he offered it to her like a present.

Sarina moaned at the invitation, taking more of him in her mouth as his hips rocked forward in an invitation too good to pass up. She opened her mouth wider and slid him in, indulging in the weight of him on her tongue. His taste was intoxicating, seductive and familiar as she sucked and teased him in turn.

Justin moved beneath her; with each stroke of her tongue he grunted and gasped, his fingers digging into her hair, pulling and leaving a shock of tingling pleasure on her scalp. He grew harder, skin tighter, his moans of pleasure louder in the silence of the treetops and Sarina reveled in her power to make him feel all these things. Giving him pleasure made her wet, the ache in her breasts, her belly, her sex building with each thrust and suck. If this was only temporary, she was going to make sure she had amazing memories to take with her.

"Sarina, stop, baby." Justin pulled away from her,

his expression half pain and half feral as he reversed their positions and flipped her underneath him.

He dipped his head, taking her mouth in a kiss that was meant to calm him—or her, she wasn't sure. She wove her fingers in his hair, opening her mouth to him, spreading her legs in a sexual invitation. Justin ground against her, the friction delicious but not enough with her clothing still between them. She whimpered in frustration and he broke off the kiss, pulling back enough to be able to look down at her.

"Sarina, I'm going to take this dress off you and then I'm not going to stop until you come." He swallowed hard, his eyes intent on her face. "If you don't want it, tell me to stop."

Sarina pushed against his chest, urging him to sit back on his knees. He complied immediately, trying hard to mask the disappointment that slid back into heated desire when she lifted the hem of her sundress and slipped it over her head.

"Does that answer your question?"

Sarina was the answer to all of his questions.

Justin knew this as sure as he knew that he would die if he didn't get inside her soon. But first he needed to explore her, taste her, make her feel a tenth of what he was experiencing right now. Sarina was usually an island unto herself, insulated from the world, and he understood why. But she let him in and now he wouldn't be satisfied until he had it all.

He inched backward off the daybed, reaching down to slip off her panties on the way down her body. He paused over her abdomen, placing soft, searching kisses along her flesh, loving the heavy inhales and exhales. Justin peered up at her, finding her eyes locked on his, intense and dark with her desire.

Sarina licked her lips and reached out to touch him but pulled back at the last moment, her swollen lips curved into a hint of a smile. He watched, riveted, as she let her fingers coast across her collarbone and in between her full breasts. She took her time, killing him slowly but he had no power to look away when she lifted a finger to her mouth, sucked on it and then used it to slowly caress a dark, hard nipple.

"Oh, you asked for this," he groaned, dragging her to the edge of the couch and spreading her wide with the breadth of his shoulders.

Justin locked his eyes on her face, soaking in every flutter of her lashes, every bite of her teeth into her lower lip, every moan that escaped her mouth. The first glancing touch of his fingertips against her clit had her moaning and biting her lip.

"No way," he murmured. "Don't hold back. I want to hear you, Sarina. You've been haunting my dreams for weeks and now I want the real thing."

The next pass of his fingertip against her clit had her throwing her head back, exposing her throat to him as her moan washed over his skin and carried across the treetops.

"Look at me, baby. Watch." Justin was patient, waiting until Sarina returned her gaze to his before he lowered his head and licked her, letting her taste explode across his tongue. His mouth watered and her hips thrust upward in an invitation he fully intended to accept. Justin was going to dive in and take his fill, try to satisfy his cravings for this woman.

There was no rush. He'd cleared his calendar for the evening and he had nowhere to be, so he took his time, in spite of the voice in his head urging him to take her now, to bury himself inside her and come. Sarina hadn't been taken care of enough in her life; she hadn't been made a priority enough. He couldn't give her forever but he could give her this now.

Sarina writhed against his mouth, pressed into the deep thrusts of his tongue, moaned and clutched his hair in a painful twist when he lavished her with sucking strokes of his tongue that ended circling her clit. She was wet and he was hard as a rock. Her legs shook with pleasure and her body shifted under him, her muscles taut and straining as she came against his mouth and shouted out her pleasure.

"Justin, fuck me," she panted out between attempts to catch her breath. "Do you have protection?"

"Yes." Justin had never been a Boy Scout but he was glad that he'd slipped a strip of condoms in his pocket before he'd come over. He hadn't been sure that anything would happen but he'd known he was at his limit of restraint with Sarina, and he'd come prepared.

He fished them out of his pocket and ripped one off, opening the wrapper with shaking fingers. He slid the condom over his length, took himself in hand and stroked the tip of his penis against the slick flesh of her sex. Sarina gasped, arching against him and trying to press down on his cock. He let her push down and watched as he entered her body; her sweet, searing heat made his eyes cross. Then he retreated, gathering up his strength to make this last.

Justin pressed in deeper, bearing down and into her, letting gravity and desire take him to the place he'd dreamed about since that night in Vegas. Sarina wrapped her arms around his neck and pulled him tighter against her body, her nails scraping the flesh of his back in long, nerve-tingling strokes. He claimed her mouth in a kiss, opening her lips with his tongue and greedily taking what he wanted, what he needed. Sarina gave as good as she got, nipping his bottom lip with her teeth as she thrust up against him, driving him deeper and deeper.

Sarina clung to him, a strangled sound of protest erupting from her when he pulled back as he started a slow, deep glide in and out of her body.

"Look at us, baby." Justin adjusted the angle to give them the perfect view of the way they moved together. He was hard and she was soft and it was agony and heaven to watch him enter and retreat, empty and fill. He needed to slow down; he needed to look away because the combination of her body and scent and the sounds of their lovemaking was driving him toward his orgasm too fast. And he wanted this to last.

But looking at her didn't work any better. Their gazes locked. Her face flushed with her passion, lips swollen with kisses, was a whole new kind of hell, the good kind. Justin leaned down, covering her body with his as she wrapped her legs around his waist, hooking her ankles together behind his back. The movement tensed her body and her sex clenched around him as he entered her again and again.

Justin slammed over and over into her heat. Deep, primal, possessive groans he could not stop erupted with each thrust as his entire world narrowed to the woman in his arms. He wanted her to come, needed her to come. He needed to be the man who brought her to the point where she let down all of the walls that kept her heart safe, that kept everyone at arm's length. Justin needed to be the only man she let in.

Her orgasm hit and he reveled in the way that she screamed his name, dug her nails into his skin, wrapped herself tighter around him. Justin sped up his thrusts, holding her even tighter as he gave in to his own orgasm, coming with a roar buried in her hair and against her sweat-damp skin.

He held her close, shifting their bodies into a tangled mess of arms and legs and tousled blankets as they both settled back into their retreat in the trees. Sarina was quiet, her eyes shut as her fingers traced sweet circles on the skin of his chest. He could feel her withdrawing from him, her brain reconstructing the walls that she'd needed to survive.

Justin didn't want her to shut him out. He knew that eventually it would happen when they both went their separate ways but he couldn't face it today. Not after what had just happened.

"Don't run, Sarina," he whispered.

"I'm right here."

"You're running away, in here." He lightly tapped a finger against her temple. "Just don't. Not tonight."

The silence dragged out between them and he waited for her to sit up and get dressed, to hurry back to her room at the house. But she didn't do any of those things. She stayed, wrapped in his arms as the stars popped up in the sky above them.

But when she did speak, it wasn't what he wanted to hear.

"I won't run tonight but it's what I do, Justin. It's what I do."

And he accepted it—for now.

Ten

"And this deal is done."

Justin pushed back from his desk, setting down his pen as his eyes scanned the three huge monitors sitting on the large surface. The screens were filled with spreadsheets, charts and computations. A few feet behind them on the wall, large TV screens featured the major news stations on mute, covering the domestic and foreign markets. The screen to the far right had a running Twitch feed of one of his favorite gamers taking down alternative civilizations in a CGI environment.

But the stuff that mattered, the stuff that he and Adam had busted their asses to make happen, was going to work. The deal with Aerospace Link was going to solidify their leadership in the future of cloud-based technology.

And it was going to make them even more ridiculously rich than they already were.

More importantly, it was going to allow them to fund and mentor other scrappy kids who dropped out of school with nothing but Red Bull-fueled dreams and a couple of laptop computers.

"Are you sure?" Adam paced across the floor in front of Justin's desk, his brows scrunched together in an intense expression. Adam was the worrier and he wasn't great with numbers, so Justin walked him through it one more time.

Numbers were as basic as breathing for Justin. When words twisted up on him and made things that came so easily to everyone else so hard for him, so hurtful, numbers had been his solace. So he gladly walked Adam through all of it and showed him exactly how their dreams were still coming true.

"And this is solid. A sure thing?" Adam asked, gesturing toward the multicolored pie chart on one screen.

"Well, nothing is guaranteed but our part is solid. Worst case —we make millions. Best case—we make levels of fuck-you money that will enable our great-great-great-great-great-great-great-grandkids to tell people to fuck off." Justin went over to his fridge and pulled out two bottles of beer, popping the tops and handing one off to his best friend. They clinked bottles and both took a long drink. "Now, normally we don't drink on the job but this is a celebration and we are done for the day."

Employees walked by just outside the glass walls of Justin's office. His space was on the same floor as Adam's but at the opposite corner. They both had windows that looked out over the lush green campus of Redhawk/Ling and he loved to watch their employees come and go from the building, enjoying lunch or coffee in the sunshine on the patios, or exercising on the trails. Standing here, shoulder to shoulder with his best friend, it was a little…incredible.

"I can't believe we're doing this," Justin said, nudging Adam with his elbow.

"I can't believe we *did* this," Adam replied, his smile huge as he waved his hand around like a sovereign viewing his subjects from the balcony of the palace. "I wouldn't have wanted to do it with anyone else."

"Me either," Justin said, his voice tight with emotion. He wasn't going to start bawling or anything but he loved the man standing next to him. He was more of a brother to him than his own blood and one day he'd tell him. Just not here in the middle of their business. He had a professional reputation to try to uphold. "Hey, Nana Orla and I want you, Tess and Roan to come over for a cookout tonight. You don't need to bring anything, we've got it covered."

"What's the occasion? Other than the obvious?" Adam asked.

Justin shrugged. "Nana Orla and I thought that Sarina would love to see you. Get a little family time." He walked over to his desk, moving aside piles of papers to find the documents he'd pulled about the center for Sarina. "She's doing so great with the kids at Rise Up, Adam. Your sister is an incredible woman. What she has done with those kids is insane. I don't know how we are ever going to find anyone to replace her." He found the folder, placing it in his briefcase so that he wouldn't forget it. When he straightened up, Adam was staring at him, a strange expression on his face. "What?"

"Are you sleeping with my sister?" Adam's voice was even, raising Justin's hackles. He couldn't tell if Adam was going to hit him or welcome him to the family. They'd never really talked about his quickie-Vegas-temporary marriage to Sarina.

It looked like it was happening now.

"Yes. I am." Justin wasn't going to lie about it. Hell, Adam would see the two of them together tonight and with one look know that they were involved. "She's my wife."

Justin closed his eyes the minute the words had left his mouth. They were true but not the ones to say.

"Not for long." Adam leveled his gaze at him, placing his beer bottle down on the table by the window. "Unless the plan to get a divorce has changed?"

"No, that plan hasn't changed."

"Then what the fuck are you doing, Justin? Sarina isn't one of the many women you cycle through your life like food that's about to expire. She's been disposable her whole life, Justin. So I'm going to ask you again—what the hell are you doing with Sarina?"

I'm falling for her.

Shit. Where did that come from? Justin rolled it around in his head, over his tongue, let it settle in the vicinity of his heart.

Nope. It wasn't romance. It wasn't feelings that lead to forever and golden wedding anniversaries. It was just a sex-induced crush on a woman he admired and respected.

Justin didn't do love and he didn't do permanent. All the women in his life prior to Sarina had known this and Sarina knew it now. This was just a longer-term hookup and he had no business confusing it with anything more than that.

But that wasn't what you told the brother of the woman you were hooking up with. Not if you wanted to live. "I care for her. She cares for me. We're friends," Justin replied, not encouraged by the tightening of Adam's jaw. "We're working it out, Adam. There's been something there since the night we met. We have…a connection. I don't know where it's going to end up but I swear to you that I'm not going to hurt her."

"You can't promise that, Justin. The only way to do that is to not get involved with her."

Justin sighed, holding his hands up in surrender. "I don't think anybody is going to get hurt. We're two adults and we both know the score."

The silence that followed was awkward. Not only because it stretched out but because Justin couldn't breathe. His chest hurt like he'd taken a stray kick in the ring at the gym.

Finally, Adam huffed out his answer, his voice equal parts pity and warning. "I don't know which one of you is the bigger fool."

Eleven

"Did you tell Adam we're sleeping together?"

Sarina pulled Justin aside, hissing the question into his ear as everyone filed down the buffet line and piled their plates with food. She'd arrived home from a day at the center and found her brothers, Nana Orla and Tess all on the patio with cold beverages and the boys fighting over who got to control the grill.

Tess had won the argument, and now she was Sarina's vote to always run the barbecue. The food was delicious.

"Adam is giving me these weird sad eyes and Roan and Tess are giving him the cut-that-out eyes and then looking at me so I can only assume that you spilled the beans with my brother-slash-your best friend," she whispered, looking over her shoulder to find Adam staring at them both, only to be nudged out of stalking mode by a poke from Tess. "What did you tell him?"

"The truth, when he asked me point-blank. I didn't think it would do anybody any good to lie about it." Justin moved over to the buffet table, grabbing a plate and adding a piece of steak and some shrimp to it. He stopped, sneaking a look over his shoulder toward her brothers and then back to her face.

Justin paused to consider something and then put down his plate, reaching for her and pulling her into a kiss. It wasn't porn-level but it was deep, intense, wet, and left no doubt that they were more than friends. Spouses with benefits?

And everyone was staring. Not that she had eyes in the back of her head but everything had gone silent around them. Even the birds had stopped chirping.

They parted and Justin rubbed his thumb against her bottom lip, pressing another quick kiss to it before picking up an empty plate and placing it in her hands.

"Eat up, baby." Justin grinned, then continued to load his plate up with grilled veggies and potatoes.

Sarina glanced over to where her family was seated, shaking her head at their reactions. Roan and Tess had their thumbs up, Adam acted like he hadn't seen anything, and Nana Orla was fanning herself with her napkin and pretending to faint on the lounger.

Sarina shook her head. "Family is weird."

When they finished filling their plates and took seats nearby, everyone decided to act like nothing had happened. She was okay with that. One hundred percent.

They ate their food, trading small talk while the sun set behind the hills and the solar lights cast a warm glow over the patio. This house was beautiful, the setting stunning, and tonight the company was perfect. Sarina soaked it in, pushing aside the somber thoughts about what they could have had if she and her brothers had grown up together instead of being separated. Would they have spent summer evenings eating hamburgers off the grill and trading inside family jokes? Would Adam and Roan have given her boyfriends the stink eye when they came to pick her up?

Would she have been braver? More willing to take a chance on what was happening between her and Justin?

Woulda. Coulda. Shoulda.

"So, Sarina, how do you like working at the center?" Tess asked, her plate balanced on her belly like a pregnancy party trick. "Adam says you're doing great."

"I love it. The kids are wonderful and so supportive of one another." She flashed appreciative glances at Adam and Justin. "You guys did an amazing thing by giving those kids that place. Giving them each other. It's something to be proud of. I hope you know that."

"I knew you'd get it," Justin answered, reaching over to cover her hand with his own. "And the kids. I knew you'd get them." He turned and winked at Adam. "We don't even rate anymore, buddy. I stopped by the other day and the first thing out of Little Pete's mouth was, 'Where's Sarina?'"

"All I got was, 'You're so lucky to have Sarina as a sister.'" Adam mimicked the big guy's booming, puberty-cracking voice. He turned his gaze toward Sarina, his smile tender and sweet enough to bring tears to her eyes. "But I have to agree with him. I'm really lucky to have you as a sister, Sarina."

She cleared her throat, trying to pull herself together. There were things she needed to say, but this wasn't the time. But she could set one thing straight. "I think I'm the lucky one." She looked between her two brothers. "I'm lucky to have both of you."

And she was lucky. Their family had been broken, torn apart by people in the system who decided that the three kids would be better off with families who could give them "a better life." They weren't the only Native kids who were taken from their parents and adopted by non-Native families, but having company didn't make the pain it had caused any easier.

But Adam had found her and Roan and now they had a chance to be a family again.

Adam and Roan exchanged a look and she wondered what was going on. Roan got up and walked over to where he'd placed his messenger bag next to the back door. He opened the flap and pulled out a small package, handing it to her when he came back to the group.

"Adam and I had some things from our folks, things we managed to keep when they split us up. I don't know how I got any of it when I was so young but it followed me around and I just stashed it away." Roan pushed a long chunk of hair behind his ear, giving her a shy smile as he handed it over. "We wanted you to have it."

She took the package, placing it on the table in front of her, squeezing her hands to stop the shaking. Justin scooted closer to her, his hand at her back, soothing and supporting. Sarina looked at him and he smiled, nodding in encouragement.

"Baby, go ahead," he whispered, nudging the package closer.

"Okay. Okay," she replied, voice shaky and thready to her own ears. With a deep breath she opened the package, sliding back the zipper and upending the bag to let all the contents slide out.

Photographs. Two of her parents. They looked happy, her mother sitting in her father's lap. One of Adam, holding a football in a Pop Warner uniform. One of two fat babies—clearly her and Roan.

Sarina covered her mouth with her hand, choking back emotion. Tears slid over her cheeks but she didn't wipe them away as she sorted through the remainder of the items.

A Christmas card signed by people whose names she didn't recognize. A beaded woven bracelet with red and black beads on a leather strap.

And a CD. Linda Ronstadt's *Living in the USA*.

"This was my mother's." She glanced up at Adam and Roan, surprised to see the tears on their faces. "This was our mother's CD. The only thing I have from our home is a copy of Linda Ronstadt's *Heart Like a Wheel*. I know it was hers because she put her name on it. I listen to it all the time." She wiped away the tears and let Justin take her hand. "My only memory is her singing to me."

"'Different Drum,'" Adam said, nodding his head in agreement. "She used to sing 'Different Drum' to us when she was trying to get us to sleep."

Sarina laughed. Really it was more of a snort joined with a weepy half sob but it was as good as it was going to get tonight. This was…a lot. Good *a lot* but…a lot.

Roan started humming the tune and Adam joined in. They were awful, tone-deaf, and any minute now Wilma was going to start barking.

Her brothers were awful but they were hers and now that she had them back, she was never going to let them go.

But she might temporarily lose them if they kept making the terrible noises they thought was music.

"If either of you start singing, I'll punch you in the face."

Justin buried deep inside her was the best part of her day.

"Deeper. Harder. Please." Sarina pulled him closer, her arms and legs wrapped around his sweat-slick body as he drove into her. It wasn't enough. She could never get enough.

It had been a long, incredible day. First, the kids at the center and the way they'd pulled together at the rock climbing wall and then the amazing dinner with her brothers, Tess and Nana Orla. The package of items from her parents had been overwhelming; she still hadn't processed all the memories that it had dredged up.

It really had been one of the best days of her life.

They'd wrapped up dinner and all she could think of was getting Justin in her room, stripping off all their clothes and making each other feel good all night long.

But it wasn't enough. Sarina strained, moaned, clutched him closer, and she needed more. Wanted more.

"Hold on, baby." Justin flipped them both over, lifting his arms and resting them over his head as he stared up at her.

It was dark in the room but his body was illuminated by a swath of moonlight pouring through the window. He was smiling at her, his eyes roaming over her face and body, his fingers flexing with his obvious desire to reach out and touch her. Take control. But he knew what she needed.

She didn't want to think about how that made her feel or what that meant.

"Baby, you take what you need."

"Justin."

"Sarina, take what you need. Use me." He reached a hand up and touched her lower lip with his fingertips. "Whatever you need, baby. I'm here for it."

She nodded, placing her hands on his chest as she began a slow glide up and down his cock. He was deep, hitting all the spots where she needed him the most. And she was in control of this, in control of her pleasure and his, when she wasn't in control of anything in her life right now.

So she took control. Riding him, taking him inside her body, clenching around him until he writhed beneath her. He kept his hands above his head, his moans and upward thrusts adding to her pleasure, the fire growing in her belly and racing along her skin. This was what she needed.

Justin. Sex. Power. Control.

The way he looked at her like she was the only person in his world.

Sarina leaned over him, joining their fingers at

the same time she joined their mouths in a kiss. His tongue tangled with hers as they moved together, faster and harder and deeper. She came, crying out her pleasure against his neck, inhaling his scent and ignoring the tears that stung her eyes.

Justin froze underneath her, his cock stiffening inside her as he shattered, crying out her name.

A million heartbeats later he shifted them over on their sides, facing the moon. She was the little spoon to his big spoon and there was nowhere she wanted to be other than wrapped up in his arms.

"Big night. The stuff Roan and Adam gave you was pretty amazing." Justin whispered against her hair, his lips brushing against her temple. "You okay?"

"I don't know." Sarina reached back to stroke his hair, laughing when he pressed a kiss against her palm. "I think I will be."

"What was the word you used with the kids at the rock climbing wall? It started with an *S*."

She thought back to that day, finally realizing what he was referring to. *"Sidanelv?"*

"Yep. *Sidanelv*." He hugged her tight. "You've got a good *sidanelv*."

She giggled at his butchering of the word but loved that he tried. "I do. Adam and Roan are great."

The house settled around them, the evening slipping into deeper night as they held each other. Sarina closed her eyes, drifting in that place between sleep and wakefulness, the place where she had it all figured out.

But she didn't have anything figured out. Not even close. And the more time she spent with Justin the easier it was to forget that this was temporary. They had a committee of lawyers making sure they never got to their first anniversary and while she and Justin were having fun with the "honeymoon" part of the marriage, the rules had not changed. Justin liked her and he liked sex with her even more but that wasn't a love match and it never would be.

Justin interrupted her thoughts, his voice scratchy with sleep. "I want to take you somewhere. As a surprise."

Sarina shook her head. "I don't like surprises."

"You'll like this one."

Twelve

"How long have you been able to fly a helicopter?"

Justin glanced over to where Sarina sat in the passenger seat of the Redhawk/Ling helicopter. Her cheeks were flushed, her eyes lit up from within with excitement. She hadn't balked at all, jumping into the passenger seat immediately and soaking in every bit of the scenery outside the front window during the flight. They weren't even at their destination and his plan was already a success, worth all the hassle he'd had to navigate to get a couple of days off.

"I learned to fly when I was twenty-three and we bought the bird last year. It's easier to get to meetings when we have our own helicopter."

"And you love it," Sarina said, her grin wide and knowing.

"I love it," he agreed. He pointed out a few dolphins swimming in the ocean below them as they headed up the coast. "You really can't beat the view."

"I have to say I'm surprised that you enjoy flying with your fear of heights. Doesn't this freak you out?" Sarina asked, watching him closely.

"Shockingly, no. I think it's because I'm in control of the machine. I'm so focused on flying that I just don't worry about it." Justin scanned the gauges, expanding on a topic he'd thought about often. "I'm dyslexic—reading is so tough for me but I can unravel numbers and math problems in my sleep. Brains are so strange, such a mystery, and mine is not the same as other people's. So how much weirder is it that I can't climb a wall but I can fly over the ocean?"

"I think your brain is pretty amazing."

Justin bit back a grin, the warmth in his belly caused by her words threatening to spill over in a laugh. "And I thought you wanted me for my body."

"Well, your ass *is* mighty fine," she teased, her voice coming through the headset as she turned away from him to look out the window. "But I think I'm more interested in your helicopter."

"Keep it up, baby. I'll just turn around and you'll never know where we're going."

She whipped back around, her face full of horror, prompting him to laugh out loud. "You wouldn't."

"Try me," Justin replied, looking over his shoulder and easing the helicopter into a turn back toward Silicon Valley. "It will be no problem to just head on back home. Wilma will be thrilled to see us."

"You don't scare me." Her lips pressed together in a frown but her voice and her side-eye glance were full of mischief.

"Well, that's good because we'll be landing in five minutes."

In spite of his ridiculous level of excitement, Justin carefully went through all of the maneuvers to get them safely on the ground. He settled it all with the staff at the heliport, turning over the keys to the helicopter and making arrangements for it to be ready in two days for their return home. The whole time he watched Sarina out of the corner of his eye, soaking in her excitement and barely contained curiosity.

Finally, he grabbed their bags and headed over to the car he'd ordered. She slid into the passenger seat and he couldn't wait another minute to end the suspense—whether for his own benefit or hers, he wasn't sure. All he knew was that he wanted to give this weekend to Sarina because she deserved it and more.

And he was beginning to realize that he wanted to give her more than a romantic weekend away; he wanted to give her the world. He wanted to give her a part of himself that he was pretty sure she'd already stolen.

It wasn't pity that drove him to want to take care of her, to make her life easier. Sarina was a survivor and had made a great life for herself. And when you got past her walls, she was generous and supportive and totally in your corner. When she told him that she believed in him he believed her. When she looked at him like he was enough and perfect just the way he was? He believed her.

That was something he'd never gotten from anyone else in his life and so Sarina deserved all the best things because she'd given the best thing to him.

But she was skittish, only comfortable in the construct of their having an end date, and she was poised to run.

And he needed more time to figure himself out. Because of one thing he was certain: he never wanted to be part of the long line of people who let Sarina Redhawk down. He just didn't know if he could be the man to break through her defenses.

Their divorce papers would arrive any day now, so the clock was ticking on his time to figure it out.

But today it was all about giving Sarina a weekend she'd never forget and a memory to last a lifetime.

"Are you going to tell me where we are? Where are we going?" Sarina asked, fastening her seat belt. "I don't like surprises."

"Really? I haven't heard that before."

Justin leaned over the middle console, tipping up

her face to kiss her. She opened to him, humming into the kiss as he drew it out, relishing the taste of her. Reluctantly, he broke it off, his excitement at getting to their final destination greater than his desire to keep kissing her.

"So, we're in Malibu," Justin revealed as he ended the kiss.

"Malibu? What's in Malibu?"

"The ocean." He started the car and pulled out of the heliport.

"Funny."

"Let me spoil you, baby. You deserve it." Justin dropped his voice lower, shamelessly using all his tools of seduction to get her to let him do this for her. Sarina's cheeks flushed, the bashful shake of her head telling him that she didn't believe she deserved it. But he knew she did; that was enough.

"Fine," she huffed out on a pout that didn't look real. He knew she was enjoying this but she'd never admit it.

They drove down the highway a few miles. Sarina focused on the scenery that whizzed past the windows: gorgeous homes, green hills, and on the one side the Pacific Ocean spreading out as far as the eye could see. He saw his landmark mile marker and pulled his next-to-last surprise out of his pocket and handed it to Sarina. She took it, shaking it out and staring at it and then Justin with a raised eyebrow.

"A blindfold?" Sarina tossed it back in his lap. "I'm not into that stuff, Justin."

"That's an interesting place you went there, Little Miss Kinky, but that's not what the blindfold is for. I want you to be completely surprised. So put it on, please." He tossed it back at her, slowing the car down as if he was going to pull over to the side of the road. "Don't make me stop the car."

"Fine," she sighed heavily and put the blindfold on over her eyes.

"You can't see anything?"

"No, Justin, I can't see anything."

"Okay, grumpy, we'll be there in five minutes." Justin navigated the traffic, turning into the Colony enclave. He rolled down the window and showed the gate guard his ID, mentioning that their final destination was a surprise for his wife. The guard winked at him and pointed to the direction he needed to drive. The directions were perfect and before he knew it they were on the right street and slowing down for the house number.

The houses were similar, many built in the 1920s and then greatly expanded in the successive decades as oceanfront property became the hottest topic in California. These houses were passed down from generation to generation, only rarely hitting the open market. The one he was looking for wasn't usually available for rent but he knew a guy who knew a guy and he asked him to help make a dream come true for his girl.

Being a billionaire absolutely had its perks.

He saw the house he was looking for and turned into the driveway, shutting off the engine and undoing his seat belt with shaking fingers. Justin couldn't believe how nervous he was; he desperately hoped that Sarina would love it. He just wanted to make her happy. It was quickly becoming the most important part of his life: making her smile and living for ways to keep her smiling.

This weekend would be big for the both of them. The divorce papers were on the way and he wasn't so sure he wanted to sign them anymore.

He had no idea how he'd arrived at this point but he knew he had to face up to the feelings he had for Sarina. Justin was scared shitless; he loved his commitment-free life and just a few short weeks ago he'd have bet all his chips that it was never going to change. And now he was more worried about Sarina signing those papers and leaving than he was about giving up his freedom.

He had no idea how Sarina felt about him but this weekend he'd find out. It was the emotional equivalent of walking out on that crazy Grand Canyon glass bridge but he was going to do it.

And he really hoped the glass didn't shatter underneath his feet.

"Stay here. I'll come around and get you," he said,

leaving their bags for later. He opened the door, taking her hand and easing her out of the vehicle. She was unsteady, her fingers gripping tightly on his arm as she found her balance. She was scowling, and so cute that he couldn't resist leaning forward and stealing a kiss. He'd meant for it to be quick, light, but he couldn't resist Sarina when she was this close. He deepened the connection, lingering, tasting and exploring, "You are addictive."

She hummed out her reaction, licking her lips and leaning toward him for more. Justin loved this part of the surprise but he missed seeing her look at him like he was the answer to all of her questions. Sarina's approval drowned out a lifetime of missing the mark on his parents' expectations and he wanted to give her everything in return. He'd start with the next couple of days and then see if they could have forever.

"Okay, hold on to me. I'll lead you inside, don't worry. I won't let you fall."

The scents in the air were already different, salty and warmed by the sunshine with a hint of sunscreen and outdoor cooking. Sarina lifted her face to the sun, head cocked to pick up nearby sounds as he guided her toward the front of the house.

He unlocked the front door and she paused, stopping briefly as the first wave of air-conditioning hit their bodies. "Okay, two more steps and then I need you to stand still while I close the door and pull back the blinds. Just wait here."

"Okay," she said. Sarina stood in place, her body adjusting to follow the sounds of his progress around the room.

He watched her closely, the anticipation building inside him like Christmas and his birthday all rolled up into one moment. Justin made his way back to her, placing his hand on her cheek, sighing when she leaned into his touch, her hands reaching out to seek him, her fingers snagging and tangling with the cotton of his T-shirt.

"Are you ready?" When she nodded, he eased around her, stopping when he stood behind her and she leaned back against his chest. Justin reached up, fingers hovering over the ties to the blindfold. "I really hope you like this. I'm going feel like an idiot if you don't."

She laughed. "Justin, you do realize that the longer you drag this out the bigger this gets and then the chances of you looking like an idiot increase?"

"Well, when you put it that way…" he huffed out in mock indignation, pulling the ties loose. "But I really do hope that you love this, baby."

The blindfold slid off and he stepped to the side so that he could watch her as she took it all in. She blinked a few times, letting her eyes adjust to the light, brushing her hair back from her eyes. Her face scrunched up in confusion and he could see the cogs of her brain working as every synapse fired in an attempt to put two and two together. She moved forward, stepping down into the sunken den that led to the wall of windows that framed the patio, the deck, and the Pacific Ocean beyond.

"Justin, this is beautiful," she said, peering at a line of black-and-white photographs on the wall. He watched as she froze, moving closer to get a better look, reaching out to trace a finger over an image. She put her face a little closer, squinting as if she didn't believe what she was looking at, and then she turned to look at him. "This is not…"

"Number thirty-eight Malibu Colony was the home of Linda Ronstadt from 1975 to 1980. She moved here just after she released *Heart Like a Wheel* and this is where they filmed her in the *Wonderland* documentary." Justin stopped, not sure how to continue. "That's all I know about her but I thought…" He faltered, feeling like an idiot now that they were here and this surprise that had felt like such a big deal in his head sounded really dumb as he was saying it out loud. "… I don't know, Sarina. I know she's one of your favorites and your mom…damn, I just thought you might like it."

Sarina was all big eyes and open mouth and looking at him like he'd lost his damn mind one minute and then she was in his arms, kissing him, and his whole world was right again.

"You *are* an idiot," she said between kisses and

laughter. "But you are the sweetest idiot I know and I don't know why you're so good to me."

"Because you deserve to get all the good things, Sarina. I don't know what's more wrong, the fact that you don't think you deserve it or that someone hasn't made it their business to ensure you always have the best of everything." Justin said it without thinking, knowing that he was revealing more than he probably should.

Sarina placed her palm on his cheek, her eyes searching his for something she needed to know. But Sarina was direct, so she just asked him.

"Do you think you're that person?"

He paused for only a minute, feeling like he was at the top of the rock wall, getting ready to take a plunge with no net beneath him. "I think I might be that person."

They stared at each other for several long minutes, both waiting for the other to say something, to do something. He took the coward's way out.

"I'm going to get the bags while you go explore."

They had a great day in Linda Ronstadt's house.

The four-bedroom beach bungalow sat right on the ocean, with only an expanse of outdoor space and large rocks to buffer it from the waves that lapped right up to the edge of the wooden deck when the tide was at its highest. Right now there was a wide swath of sand, full of people running, children playing and neighbors enjoying the gorgeous California sunshine. A private beach, it wasn't crowded, and Sarina was easy to find once he'd moved the luggage into the gorgeous master bedroom on the second floor.

Swimming. A long walk on the sand. It was a perfect day that led to a perfect dinner. Shrimp and lobster, grilled to perfection with vegetables and the perfect bottle of wine on the deck, under the stars. Now they were full, skin warm from hours in the sun, and just the two of them talking about nothing and everything.

Except the one thing he couldn't get the nerve to ask her because if the answer was that she still wanted to leave, he didn't want to hear it. Not today. They had all the time in the world to mess this up, to walk away from something that was really great.

"Top three things you love to eat," Justin said, refilling her wineglass.

"What? Are we playing some weird version of twenty questions?" Sarina leaned back in her chair, long bare legs extended with her feet in his lap.

"Yes, we are. It is my incredibly transparent attempt to get you to tell me more about yourself," Justin replied, running his hand up her calf, admiring the way her mini sundress fell off her shoulder. She was so damn sexy and didn't even know it. He knew a dozen women in LA who spent the price of a small car to look the way that Sarina did without even trying. "Would you divulge all of your secrets if I just asked you flat out?"

"Probably not."

"So indulge me. I don't think there has ever been a husband in the history of husbands who knew so little about his wife."

She stared at him over the rim of her wineglass, shaking her head at him and trying to hide a smile. "Okay, fine. Top three favorite foods…a rare steak, cotton candy and MRE beef Stroganoff."

He cocked his head at her. "MRE? Like a military meal that you shake and heat up?"

"Yep. Most of them were awful but I really loved that one." Sarina pointed to him. "Your turn."

"So, easy. Nana Orla's corned beef, my father's *youtiao* and shrimp scampi."

"What's *youtiao*?"

"It's like a fried breakfast doughnut except that it's a stick, two sticks connected, not a ring. He made them on our birthday and holidays." He chuckled. "I think it was one of the only times that fried foods were allowed in the house."

"You need to make that for me."

"Only for your birthday. When *is* your birthday?" He sat up, realizing that he had no idea.

"September second." Sarina raised an eyebrow in question. "Yours?"

"March twenty-first." He stood, holding his hand out to her. "Do you want to dance?"

She shook her head, taking his hand and standing, looking him right in the eye. "No."

"No?"

"Let's go to bed," she said, leaning forward to kiss him. Her lips were soft, tasting of the wine and the intoxicating flavor of Sarina. "I think I know everything I need to know."

Justin knew only one thing: that he needed Sarina Redhawk like he needed his next breath. He pulled her close, taking her mouth in a kiss that was full of everything he was feeling, everything she made him want and need. He didn't want it from just anyone, he wanted it from her and only her.

She tasted like secrets and risk and the forbidden, but she felt like home and the future in his arms. She was perfect for him and she was his. Now he just needed to figure out how to keep her.

Justin ran his hand over the bare skin of her shoulder, catching the thin little strap of her sundress and lowering it slowly, only stopping when her breast was bare to him. He leaned down, taking her nipple in his mouth, sucking on it with a moan, circling the puckered tip with his tongue. Sarina's hands wove into his hair, gasping as she kept his mouth exactly where they both wanted it to be.

"Take me upstairs, Justin. I want you naked, now. I need you. Please."

She would never have to ask him twice.

Justin leaned over, picking Sarina up and carrying her over his shoulder. She gasped, laughing out loud as the snagged the bottle of wine on their way to the stairs.

"You're going to drop me," Sarina protested, her fingers squeezing his ass cheeks as he mounted the stairs.

"If you keep playing with my ass I can guarantee that I'm going to drop you on yours," he half joked as he arrived on the second floor, entered the bedroom and placed her on the floor.

Sarina took the wine from his hand and put it on the side table, turning to give him a sexy, lingering once-over. When she straightened, she took one finger and hooked it under a sundress strap and lowered it, then did the same on the other side.

The tiny little sundress slithered down her body and pooled on the floor at her feet. She was naked, skin glowing in the low lights of the room, her body long and lean and mouthwateringly beautiful.

Justin let out a wolf whistle. "You are the most gorgeous woman I've ever seen."

Sarina moved forward, stopping right in front of him, and began unfastening his shorts. Her eyes were dark with her desire, her smile full of challenge. "Prove it."

Thirteen

Issuing Justin Ling a challenge was the best idea she'd ever had.

Her husband was kind, mischievous, challenging, outspoken, dedicated, romantic and sexy. She still couldn't believe that he was still available, that a woman hadn't snatched him up and put a ring on it before now.

But she wasn't any different from any of the women who'd cycled in and out of his bed before. She hadn't put a ring on it—at least she hadn't put one on again after ditching him the morning after their wedding.

And now she needed to decide if she wanted to see that ring back on her finger for good.

She'd worry about that later. After about a dozen orgasms.

Because what crazy woman would get bogged down thinking deep thoughts when Justin was standing in front of her completely naked?

"I love your body," she said, taking her time checking him out. He was so fit, his muscles under skin so smooth and tan from days spent in the California sun that all she wanted to do was taste him all over.

So she did.

Sarina slowly dropped to her knees, tracing a path down his body with her lips, pressing openmouthed kisses across his collarbone, just under his heart, on his stomach, and landing at the top of his dark treasure trail. She looked up at him, placing her hands on his thighs and offering herself to him.

"You're going to kill me," Justin murmured, taking his cock in his hand and offering it to her.

Sarina took him in her mouth, tongue caressing the long length of him, closing her eyes and savoring the pleasure it brought her to draw out his moans of desire and gasps of surrender. She opened her eyes and found him gazing down at her, his eyes dark with his passion but lit with the feelings she knew he had for her. Unspoken but there nonetheless.

She recognized it because she also felt it, knew it to be true in her heart, deeper in her soul.

It was something she'd never had before. It was

precious, fragile, but also stronger than she would have thought possible with her brokenness.

He groaned above her, his thighs trembling under her hands as he struggled for control, and suddenly she wanted nothing more than to be under his control, under his body.

She released him, standing on knees liquid with her own desire. Justin took her face in his hands, the calluses on his palms abrasive against her skin, igniting sparks of need in her blood, making her wet and hot and heavy for him. He kissed her slowly, deeply, tenderly—in total contrast to the slide of their bodies, the sweat-slick friction of hard body against soft skin, smooth flesh against coarse hair.

"Lie down on the bed," Justin ordered, his tone fierce with need.

Sarina walked backward, maintaining eye contact as she complied with the gentle command. The sheets were cool on her heated skin, silky against the back of her knees, her thighs.

Justin covered her with his body, kissing her mouth and then traveling lower to press kisses along her jaw, down her neck, into the shallow between her collarbones, lower still to the valley between her aching breasts. He layered them with kisses, the merest whisper of lips along the swell of each, until she writhed beneath him, her fingers clutching his back with long scrapes of her nails.

Justin finally claimed her nipples, licking, sucking, swirling them with his tongue until she was wet and needy between her thighs. He shifted on top of her, his fingertips trailing along the tender, sensitive skin of her thighs upward until he stroked her wet folds, finding her clit and rubbing it in small, firm circles.

"Oh, yes. Please." Sarina opened her legs wider, arm thrown over her eyes, lower lip bitten as she fought the sensation he drew out of her, as she gave in to the sensations he created inside her.

"I can do better than that," Justin murmured, releasing her breast and easing down her body with single-minded determination. "So much better."

She watched as he lowered his head between her legs, his broad shoulders opening her even wider. Justin kissed her wet folds, his tongue swirling around her clit, inside her heat, his attention's sole purpose to bring her pleasure. Justin was on his knees, but he was in control and she was completely subject to his power.

She writhed under him, thrusting herself against his face, riding his tongue, his mouth, straining for the orgasm teasing along the edges of her electrified nerve endings. Every time she got close, Justin changed his angle, pressure, intensity. He kept her on the edge, so close that when it hit, she cried out in surprise and relief. The pleasure hit her with its expected ferocity and she lurched forward, draping herself over the broad expanse of his back as she pulsed and shook with pleasure.

Sarina collapsed against the mattress, gasping for air and clutching at him when he moved over her, his body covering her as he took her mouth in a sex-flavored kiss. He stared down at her, his eyes dark and hot, molten pools of whiskey-colored lava that she could not ignore, could not break away from.

Justin broke contact only long enough to put on a condom, easing it down the length of him with sure strokes.

"Sarina, I want you so much." His chest heaved with each of his labored breaths, body taut with desire. "I'm going to fuck you until you come again because I can't get enough of it. I can't get enough of you."

"Please, Justin. I need you inside me. Please." She knew she was begging and she didn't care. She held so much of herself back from everyone but she couldn't do that here, not in this bed. They might not know what the future held for them but when they were together like this, they were infinite. They were complete; just the two of them were perfection. She didn't want to ruin that, didn't want reality to intrude.

Justin groaned at her words, and his fingers dug painfully into her hips as he dragged her forward and positioned her over his hard cock. He trembled and she thrilled at the power that she had over this man. But his words shook her control.

"Sarina, I want you to come for me. Getting you off, feeling your body grip me so tight, hearing the whimpers and sounds you make for me, just for me, keeps me up at night. I can't stop thinking about you. I want you all the time and I need to know that I'm not alone in this." Justin reached down between them and grabbed his dick, pushing inside her and joining them in the best way possible. She moaned, bucking up with a flare of pleasure when he began a slow, deliberate circle of the pad of his thumb over her clit. "Don't leave me alone in this, Sarina. Show me that you're here with me. Show me that you feel what I feel."

She couldn't have denied him even if she wanted to. Justin was so open, so vulnerable in this moment, so raw and naked. Not just in the physical sense. They were both stripped bare and even if she wanted to deny him, she couldn't. If she tried to hold it in she'd explode with the intensity, come apart in a way she was afraid would leave nothing of her remaining. So she opened herself to him; her body, her heart. She let him have all of her.

Justin drove into her, his cock moving in deep as she pushed back against him, struggling and straining to get even closer. She was playing with fire, she knew, and she wasn't the risk-taker. Nothing was settled between them and the voice telling her to run was getting louder and louder in her head. She knew that if she left, Justin would move on and fill his life and his bed with someone who was better suited for him. She just wanted this for tonight.

"Sarina, I need you," Justin moaned on a deep thrust, his body covering hers as he took her hands and lifted them over her head. Their fingers tangled together, bodies moving in the same rhythm, their heartbeats and the thrust and retreat of their bodies in perfect synchronicity.

Sarina looked up at him, letting him take over as her orgasm built tighter and hotter in her belly. Justin thrust deeper, harder, groaning his desire out between clenched teeth. Their skin was slick with sweat as they pressed against each other and his hardness rubbed against her clit with every stroke.

"Sarina, please."

She tightened her legs around him. The orgasm was building inside her, up from the base of her spine, making her legs shake and grow weak with the effort. It was terrifying, this all-consuming need, and she fought the urge to disengage her body, her heart, to run from this man.

Justin leaned down, his lips brushing her, his tongue exploring her mouth. He ended the kiss, whispering, "Don't run."

Sarina gasped out loud, her arms breaking free from his grip to wrap around his neck and hold him against her as she came. Justin's cock drove inside her one last time and his muscles shook with the impact of his orgasm. His fingers wove into her hair, clutching and releasing as his body came down.

Justin moved to shift off her, complaining quietly that he was hurting her, but she shook her head. She wrapped herself tighter around him, wanting to draw this moment out as long as she possibly could.

Justin wanted more, that message was coming through loud and clear. And she wanted it too. But she was afraid. Terrified.

She'd been wanted by people before and they'd rejected her in the end, sending her back into the system. She'd learned to not need anyone, to reject them before they pushed her to the side. She ran— it was what she did—and now she had to decide if she was willing to stay and see if the risk was worth the reward.

They were spooning again. This was quickly becoming one of her favorite ways to spend the hours of quiet between the busyness of the day and stillness of the night. The stars outside the open French doors of the bedroom were better than anything on TV and Justin was warm, strong and surrounding her as if he wanted to protect her from the world. She wanted to let him.

"Thank you for this, Justin." The words weren't enough but they were all she had.

"I wanted to do something for you." He kissed her shoulder, spanning his hand across her body in a gesture that made her chest tighten and warm with emotion. "It was risky. I wasn't sure if you would like it or not."

She rushed in to reassure him; the vulnerability in his tone wasn't something he allowed to come through very often. "I loved it. This has been the best day." Sarina peeked over her shoulder at him, taking his hand and weaving their fingers together. "You're good with risks. You take them. It's better than not taking any at all."

"Being cautious isn't a character flaw," he said, his breath stirring her hair, warming the back of her neck. "I know people wish I was more careful."

"Sometimes being cautious feels a little like being the walking dead. It's like standing on the edge of the game but never going in."

"You're braver than you realize."

"If I were brave, I'd say that we need to talk about it…about us. My bike is fixed. The divorce papers have arrived."

His fingers tightened on her hand and his heart-beat started a hammer against her back. "Are we going to talk about it?"

She rolled his question over in her mind, letting the sound of the waves as they eased in and out on the sand and the rocks below soothe her fear. They needed to talk, needed to get things settled between them. Now was the time.

But she didn't want to lose this, lose this moment.

She'd learned over the years to take each moment as it came. She didn't give the bad ones the power to take more of her than the time she had to endure them, and the good ones were places she could be fully in the moment.

And this moment, this weekend, was the best of her life and she was too scared to end it too soon.

She didn't want anything to spoil it.

She wasn't so brave after all.

"Not tonight," she murmured, drawing him closer. "Not tonight."

Fourteen

The Mountain Winery was the perfect place to hold a celebration gala.

The historic location in the mountains of Saratoga, California, was part of the Paul Masson company. It hosted weddings, corporate events, concerts and wine tastings. Redhawk/Ling had rented the entire place for the party to celebrate signing the deal with Aerospace Link. Tonight, not only Redhawk/Ling employees but also the staffs of their new business partners would mix and mingle to live music and multiple open bars.

It was not a cheap evening but Adam and Justin weren't guys who skimped on the good times when their employees busted their asses.

Sarina walked into the massive space with Nana Orla, Tess and Roan and realized that finding their hosts was going to be the great mission of the evening. Sarina was anxious to see Justin; the week since they had returned from Malibu had been hectic for him as he finalized this deal and he'd slid into bed late every night. She missed him. So much.

But it had given her a lot of time to think about them and tonight was the night she was going to tell him that she was ready to take a chance on them. She didn't want to sign the divorce papers. Sarina was ready to stop running.

She was scared but he was worth the risk.

"This place is huge," Sarina said, hanging on tight to Nana Orla. The crowd was bustling and although she was a tough lady, Sarina didn't want her trampled on her watch. "I'm going to text Justin and see where the hell they are."

"I just sent a text to Adam," Tess replied, waving her phone in the air. "Nothing yet. I'm sure they're both busy wining and dining their new best friends at Aerospace Link. We won't see them until they are dancing on top of some wine barrels or something."

"No way," Roan said, looking the women over and punctuating his appraisal with a definite thumbs-up. "You girls are smokin' and there is no way that Adam and Justin are going to let you just wander around a party with a bunch of drunk idiots hitting on you."

"What about me?" Nana Orla asked, a hand placed

on her hip while she made the what-am-I-chopped-liver gesture with her free hand. "I didn't spend three hours at the salon today to get ignored by all the hot guys at this party."

"Since you're my date tonight," Roan replied, looping her arm through his, "all these guys better just back off."

"That's fine but if I give you the signal to go away, do it. I don't want you to ruin my game," Nana Orla teased.

"Your wish is my command."

"Excuse me, Ms. Redhawk? Miss Lynch?" A young guy with glasses and an earpiece carrying a clipboard approached them and gestured toward a waiting golf cart. "I'm Evan. Mr. Redhawk and Mr. Ling arranged for transportation to take all of you to the VIP section on the Vista Deck."

"You don't have to ask me twice," Nana Orla said, making her way to the empty cart. "Take me to the open bar, young man."

"Yes, ma'am." Evan smiled, waiting until they were all settled before starting the machine and slowly navigating the crowds of people wandering around in all kinds of party clothes.

Sarina took in the entire property, comparing the reality with the photos she'd viewed on the internet. It really was a large place and she was glad she didn't have to walk all this way in the ridiculously

high heels she'd chosen for the evening. They were
sexy as hell but they weren't walking shoes.

They passed several terraces and open-air spaces,
strewn with fairy lights and dotted with tables groaning with food and bartenders making every cocktail known to man. People were dancing, laughing,
enjoying their success after having worked so hard
the previous months. If this didn't make them all
loyal employees, Sarina wasn't sure what would do
the trick.

They passed the large amphitheater-style concert
venue, with its Spanish-inspired decor lit up with col-
ored lights. A local band with a huge following was
playing a live show and the seats were packed with
bodies swaying back and forth to the tunes. Sarina
would have to convince Justin to come back here
later and catch some of the show.

The golf cart turned a corner and directly in front
of them, the area marked as the Vista Deck, was an
area cordoned off by a velvet rope and monitored by
a really big guy holding a clipboard.

Evan stopped the cart and they all piled out, offering him smiles and waves as Roan slipped him a
business card with his cell phone written on the back.

"Did you just hit on Evan?" Sarina asked, turning her head to catch the guy still checking out her
brother.

"He was adorable. Why not?" Roan shrugged,

approaching the bouncer with the clipboard and giving their names.

They passed the test with flying colors and were
all admitted into the exclusive area of the party.
There were lots of people here as well, but they were
better dressed and the waiters came to you for your
food and drink orders, no waiting in lines.

Sarina checked out the women in the section,
noting the sexy, sparkly dresses they were wearing. These women were glamorous, dressed like
movie stars, and she was thankful she'd gone with
Nana Orla and Tess to the salon and had her hair
and makeup done. Even with the best that money
could buy in beauty preparation, she was no match
for these women.

"There they are." Tess pointed to an area just to
the right where Adam and Justin were standing and
talking to a number of people whose clothes and
jewelry proclaimed that they were definitely rich
and maybe famous.

Adam was dressed all in black, his resemblance
to Roan so pronounced at this angle. Sarina's breath
caught at the way they both resembled their father,
the dark hair and high cheekbones making them ridiculously handsome.

And then she saw Justin, in dark pants and a
white button-down shirt with the sleeves rolled up.
He was the epitome of everything she thought was
sexy. Strong, masculine, confident, charming—he

made her smile and her chest tighten with an emotion she'd never really felt before.

In Malibu she'd asked him to wait to talk about their future, fear making her put off accepting what she wanted. But standing here, watching him and feeling the pull of her body and soul toward him, she knew what she wanted.

Justin.

A future together.

She wanted to remain Mrs. Ling.

And then he looked over and did an honest-to-God double take as their eyes met and she knew that he wanted the same thing. No words could have convinced her, but that look, that absolute and immediate connection between the two of them, told her what an entire dictionary full of words would never be able to tell her: Justin wanted her, too.

She started walking, grinning like an idiot with every step she took across the stone pavers to meet Justin halfway. He was smiling, too, giving his lips a sexy curve as he perused her body with eyes full of desire. And just like that, she knew she'd chosen the right thing to wear.

"You're beautiful," he breathed as soon as they were close enough not to be overheard.

They'd decided not to publicize their involvement tonight. The journalists would latch onto any whisper of a new woman in Justin's life and with nothing settled between them, she'd been wary of any attention. It had been the right decision. She was already nervous about this event and didn't need the extra pressure.

But it was damn hard not to kiss him, not to touch him.

"This old thing?" she replied, looking down at the black jumpsuit with its plunging neckline and almost nonexistent back.

"I can't wait to take it off you later," he replied, his fingers lightly brushing against the inside of her wrist, sending lightning up her arm and racing across her skin. She shivered with the impact of his touch. "Are you cold?"

She didn't get to answer, interrupted by the approach of one of the most beautiful women she'd ever seen. This woman was stunning, tall and willowy with her blond hair in loose curls falling around her tan shoulders. She wore very little makeup, her skin dewy and fresh, lashes long, and lips stained with a red gloss. This woman was the epitome of a California girl, the kind of woman men dreamed about and boys had on posters in their rooms.

"Justin, your parents want you to meet their friends from the hospital board," the woman said, her hand grasping his so easily that Sarina knew it wasn't the first time. Her eyes got wide when she saw Sarina standing there, her expression immediately apologetic. "I'm so sorry, I interrupted you. Forgive me."

Great. And she was nice, too. Sarina was good at reading people and nothing about this woman rang false.

Justin gestured between the two women, deftly removing his hand from the other woman's grasp. "Sarina Redhawk, this is Heather Scarborough."

"It's nice to meet you," they replied at the same time, causing them both to stutter and smile awkwardly.

"Oh, good. You found him." Mrs. Ling appeared over Justin's other shoulder as if she'd been conjured out of Sarina's most awkward nightmares, and the older woman's smile faltered when her gaze landed on Sarina. "Hello, Sarina. It's nice to see you here." She turned to Justin and gestured over to the other side of the space. "Justin, I need you to come and meet some people from the hospital board."

"Mom, I was just going to dance with Sarina. I'll meet them later," Justin answered, his tone tired. He held his hand out to her, his smile apologetic. "Come on."

Sarina placed her hand in his, relieved to have a few more moments alone with him, but they were stopped by the arrival of a man at their side. She didn't recognize him and by the look on Justin's face, he didn't know him either.

"Mr. Ling, Tim Gilbert from *Celebrity News.* I'm writing an article and I was hoping to get a quote."

The man punctuated his question by shoving a digital recorder in their faces.

The *Celebrity News* was a trashy tabloid specializing in gossip and half-truths that barely kept on the right side of slander. This was not a good thing and the tension in Justin's body told her that he knew it.

"I'm sorry, Mr. Gilbert, but we'll be answering questions about the new deal at the press conference in a couple of days. I'll be happy to talk to you then. If you'll excuse me, we're off to dance." Justin nodded at the man with a smile and moved to go around him but the guy fell back and blocked their path.

"I'm not interested in the new deal, Mr. Ling. I was hoping you could talk to me about your secret marriage to Sarina Redhawk."

Fifteen

"Justin, what is this man talking about?" his mother demanded, her raised voice drawing the attention of nearby VIPs.

Justin closed his eyes, knowing that he should have seen this coming. He'd been congratulating himself that they'd pulled it off, that they would be able to sneak off for a couple more days and plan their future together and then announce it to the world on their terms. And now they were exactly where he didn't want to be at the worst possible time.

So close and yet not even in the damn zip code.

"Mr. Ling, I'd like to give you and Ms. Redhawk… Mrs. Ling—" the reporter turned to smile at Sarina "—the chance to tell your story."

"I'm not going to talk to you about this here," Justin replied, pointing toward the exit and the bouncer. "Call my office and we'll schedule an interview at a better time."

"It's not going to work like that, Mr. Ling. I'm sorry. I'm going to run with this story tomorrow, with or without your comment."

Justin looked around them. They were starting to draw the attention of the crowd in the VIP area and his mother continuing to ask what was going on was not helping. His father approached, closely followed by Adam and three of the investors. He had to do damage control and he had to do it fast.

"Justin, what is he talking about?" his mother repeated, her voice filling in the silence that developed whenever people sensed a scandal looming on the horizon. "Tell him that you are *not* married to Sarina!"

"I can't do that, Ma."

The reporter smiled, the triumphant grin of a man who had a solid story that he'd file by midnight.

"So, can you confirm that you two were married in a Vegas quickie wedding? Witnesses say that you were drunk and that you both stated that you had only met a few hours before. Is that correct, Mr. Ling? Ms. Redhawk? Did you guys get married when you were total strangers and drunk? What do you plan on doing about it? We heard that you've hired divorce lawyers to end the marriage on the down low. Keep it out of the press. Although nobody would be surprised about it with your reputation, right, Mr. Ling?"

If possible, their audience got even quieter as they all processed that information. Justin couldn't blame them; this was good stuff. Better than reality TV. Did they have a popcorn station at this party? They should.

Justin motioned for the bouncer to take care of this problem. "Get this guy out of here, now."

The reporter went quietly if not entirely willingly, his expression smug. He didn't need their statement and so he wasn't going to make a fuss to stick around until he got it. His removal did little to dissolve the crowd although Roan and Adam tried to get people to give Sarina and Justin some privacy. In the end he still had his parents and several investors standing by and waiting for answers.

This time it was his father's turn to ask the million-dollar question. "Justin, is any of this true?"

The question was echoed by two of Aerospace Link's highest executives, their frowns telling him exactly what they expected his answer to be.

Justin looked at Sarina, unable to gauge where she was with this. Her face was blank, the old Sarina back in place. The one who gave away nothing and had walls that nobody could climb.

He wished that they'd had their talk because he

didn't know where she was on all of this. The last time they'd talked about it they were getting divorced and she'd avoided any discussion about a change in status since then. Justin knew she cared about him, and he knew that she enjoyed sex with him, and he knew that she still planned to get on her bike and leave him behind once the ink was dry on the divorce papers.

And he knew that a couple thousand people were here celebrating a deal that would guarantee that employees still had jobs and Redhawk/Ling could survive any downturn in the tech sector. He knew this deal was security for many people and he knew he couldn't kill it at the eleventh hour.

What he didn't know was if his wife loved him enough to stay.

He couldn't make a grand statement that they were in love and staying married when he didn't know if Sarina was willing to play along with that story. Because that couldn't be a short-term thing. It would have to be a long-haul commitment to convince everyone that it was the truth and as far as he knew, she was still going to sign those divorce papers.

So, he really had no choice. He didn't have a winning hand and it was time to fold.

Sarina would understand. He'd make her understand. It was time for him to do some damage control.

"Look, I'm married…we're married…but it was a mistake and we are in the process of having the marriage dissolved." He reached for Sarina's hand and she let him take it, but it was cold and her body was stiff. "We are committed to staying friends and remaining in each other's lives in the future. We are both part of the Redhawk/Ling family and that is how it will remain even though we will no longer be married."

"Excuse me, I think you've got this. I'm leaving." Sarina ripped her hand away from him and turned, pushing her way through the crowd and heading toward the exit.

Roan and Tess followed in her wake, their withering looks of disappointment unmistakable. Adam stayed behind but he was pissed, anger setting his jaw in a hard line and his eyes almost black with his emotion. Justin looked behind him one more time, watching Sarina's retreat, and suddenly he didn't care—he had to talk to her.

"Sarina, wait!"

His father's grip on his arm, firm and strong, stopped him in his tracks. His tone was brittle, voice deep and loud enough for only Justin to hear, but it sounded like a gunshot going off in his brain. "Justin, where are you going? Let her go. Don't throw this away right now, son. You need to keep your priorities straight and at this moment your priority *has* to be your company."

His father cast a meaningful glance at the investors, who were talking quietly together in a group, throwing the occasional skeptical glance in his direction. Nothing about their demeanor said that they were holding him or Redhawk/Ling in high regard. Everything about them said that he'd fucked up and needed to fix it—now.

His father continued. "Justin, you're always trying to tell me that I don't understand or respect your business and your accomplishments. You're wrong. I do respect your work ethic, but I think your personal life leaves a lot to be desired. You're reckless but I wouldn't care if it just impacted your personal life. You do what you want and then get offended when your poor choices jeopardize your business." His father gestured around, his movement meant to encompass all of the guests enjoying themselves at the party. "You have a lot of people who depend on you to do the right thing, to be the right thing. And I'm presuming that your new partners have insisted on the standard morality clauses?" He didn't wait for Justin to confirm it; a businessman in his own right, he already knew the answer. "So be the man these people can depend on and fix this. You are the only one who can fix this."

Justin looked in the direction where Sarina had disappeared, wishing he could do what he wanted but knowing he had to do the right thing. He'd created this mess and his father was right: he was the only one who could fix it.

He'd make this right and then he'd find Sarina and fix their forever.

Sixteen

Sarina was used to packing light and fast.

Years of moving from foster care situation to foster care situation with nothing but a few things thrown in a plastic trash bag had prepared her for the military. The army had perfected her ability to move quickly and disappear when she wanted to be gone.

She'd left the party after that humiliating fiasco and ordered the car to take her back to Nana Orla's as fast as it could without getting pulled over by the police. She'd barely set foot in the house before Wilma was growling at her. And not fifteen minutes after that, Sarina heard a car pull up outside the house and Nana Orla burst through the door on full alert, wanting to know if everything was okay.

But Sarina couldn't answer her. How could she talk about the moment when she'd been humiliated in front of the press and all of Justin and Adam's rich friends? She'd known that going to the party was a bad idea but she'd been fooled by Justin, blinded by what she felt for him.

Stupid, stupid girl.

Sarina wiped at her eyes, refusing to let the tears fall. It had been years since she'd cried over something as stupid as a guy or having her feelings hurt. She'd cried over dead men and women in the desert, so far from home and family. She'd cried as a child, missing her mom and dad and her brothers, confused by being surrounded by strangers.

She wasn't going to cry over Justin Ling.

Sarina stripped off her jumpsuit, throwing it over the chair in the room. She wouldn't need it where she was going and it would take up space in her backpack. She was back to being Sarina, finally awakened from the spell that she belonged in a world of money and power and privilege. She didn't belong in that world. She didn't belong with Justin. She'd just forgotten that for a while.

Wilma paced the floor, sensing her agitation and whining with her own anxiety. Sarina scooped her up, speaking soothingly to the dog as she showed her that she was going with her.

"Don't worry, baby." Sarina pressed a kiss to the dog's head, nuzzling against her when Wilma pressed into her body. "Look, I'm putting your toys in the bag. You're going with me. You always go with me."

"I'm going to miss the wee dog. She's mean as a snake but I love her anyway."

Sarina turned to find Nana Orla standing in the doorway. She'd changed into her nightclothes; her robe was teal tonight, embroidered with flowers and edged with multicolored pom-pom trim. It was eye-wateringly bright, but suited her with its loud and cheerful colors and design. Sarina was going to miss Nana Orla's outfits; they were a never-ending source of curiosity for her.

"You two get along because you're both little and you both bite," Sarina said, her smile hopefully conveying how much she cared for this woman. She approached Nana Orla and handed her the little dog, who went with copious wiggles and kisses. Man, leaving this time was going to hurt. Not only leaving Justin but saying goodbye to Nana Orla and Adam and Tess…these people were going to be hard to let go.

But it wasn't letting go. Not really. Her brothers would understand that she had to go and they'd support her. Their bond was new but it was strong and she knew they'd give her time to figure out her future because they were destined to be a part of it.

"Well, that's true enough, I guess." Orla entered the room, eyeing the half-packed bag and the chaos of clothing strewn all over the floor. "You can leave your things here if they don't fit in your bags. I'll keep them for you until you come back home."

Home.

Oh hell. Sarina turned from her, biting the inside of her cheek to stop the tears that threatened to spill over onto her cheeks.

"That's really sweet but I don't think I'll be back." She cut off the words *anytime soon* because they sat on the edge of her tongue, poised to add a caveat and hedge on the decision she knew she had to make. This needed to be the last time she came here, at least until she could get over the ache in her chest that throbbed every time she thought of Justin.

Home. Justin had become that place for her. She couldn't pinpoint the exact moment it had happened, but she couldn't deny it and now she had to figure out her exit plan. Time and distance would help her get over him.

"This is your home, girl." Nana Orla's voice was soft but firm, the Irish brogue wrapping around Sarina like a warm blanket. The older woman moved in close, locking eyes with Sarina before she spoke. "You know better than anyone that family is not just blood and DNA, it's the people you choose. What Justin did, it doesn't change the fact that you and I are family and always will be." The older woman reached out and placed a hand on Sarina's cheek. Her touch was warm but the surge of emotion, of love, that Sarina felt for her was enough to loosen the tears and important enough that she didn't care. "I choose you, Sarina. You and I will always be family."

"She's right, Sarina."

They both turned to find Adam standing in the doorway. He was still dressed in his tux, a tense expression on his face. He smiled apologetically at Nana Orla.

"I used the key you gave me," he explained, his gaze drifting back to Sarina. "How are you doing?"

She could feel the big-brother protectiveness rolling off him in waves and for once it didn't piss her off. It made her feel wanted, included. When he walked over to her and pulled her into a tight hug, she didn't fight him but hugged him back. Tighter. Harder. She was going to be gone for a while and she needed to make this one count, make it one she would remember.

"I'm doing better now," she admitted, surprising the both of them with her honesty. Adam went still for a moment and then he pulled her in tighter, pressing a kiss to her hair. "But I've got to go, Adam. I'm sorry."

He released her, looking down at her, clearly gauging how successful he would be if he tried to change her mind. She shook her head, wishing that this could be different. "Adam, you know I can't stay. This thing with Justin, it got complicated and so real, so fast. I have to go to get my head straight, to figure things out."

"You can't outrun these feelings, Sarina. You love him. That isn't just going to go away just because you have a few states in between the two of you."

"I know, Adam. But I need time to put this behind me. I need to find a place where I can land and stay, build a life." Sarina glanced at Nana Orla, wishing that this could be different. "I thought it might be here but I was wrong. This way I can move on and so can Justin."

"Justin is being an ass," Nana Orla said, setting Wilma on the bed. "I still can't believe what he said to that reporter."

"Look, he told them the truth," Sarina broke in, needing to make sure that they all understood exactly what had gone down between her and Justin. "Justin and I never changed our plans. He didn't betray me with what he said tonight because he was absolutely correct. I just made the mistake of thinking that things were going to be different without saying or hearing the words. The only thing we're guilty of is getting caught up in our feelings, in the emotions of the moment."

"I know what I know, Sarina," Nana Orla insisted. "I know that you love Justin and he loves you."

Sarina didn't deny it. She wouldn't disrespect what had happened between them. It was real and it was powerful. It just wasn't forever.

"But that doesn't change the truth of the matter. His parents are right—I'm not the girl for Justin. It's that simple."

"You can't just give up, Sarina," Adam said, his voice pleading. "Don't give up on Justin. Don't give up on us."

Oh no. She couldn't let him think that this had anything to do with them. "Adam, no, we're good." She swallowed hard, realizing that there were things she needed to say this man, the brother who had loved her enough to never stop looking for her. "You're my family, my brother. My *agido*. And I have never thanked you for finding me. I have never thanked you for looking for me and not giving up. All I ever wanted was to be the person who mattered to someone, a person worth remembering. A person worth missing. You gave me that. I'm prickly and stubborn but I love you, Adam. Nothing will ever change that, not ever again."

"Damn, Sarina, it took you long enough. I love you, too," Adam said, tears streaming down his face as he pulled her to him again for a longer and tighter hug. She was going to miss this. She was going to miss her brother.

She considered staying and just dodging Justin but she couldn't face that prospect. It would take longer to get over him if she stayed, and she *needed* to get over him. Distance and time would give her the strength to watch him forget about her and move on to the next woman. It wasn't brave but it was reality. Running wasn't always a bad thing. Sometimes the best defense was an organized retreat.

And this wasn't going to get any easier the longer she dragged it out. Sarina needed to go and she needed to go now.

But there was one thing she needed to do first. Sarina pushed on Adam's chest, laughing softly when he refused to let her go. After a long moment, he finally did, grumbling in protest. She walked over to the desk in the corner of the room and picked up a manila envelope, sliding out the papers and flipping to the one with the "sign here" sticky note on it. She didn't need to read the document. She'd read it a million times; the words never changed.

Those words put an end to the first time she ever dared to believe she could have the happily-ever-after. The first time in a long time she'd allowed herself to think that she could be someone's everything, the person they couldn't leave behind.

Sarina picked up a pen from the desk and weighed it in her hand. Then she signed her name.

It was that simple. A few strokes of black ink and she broke her own heart.

Sarina gathered the papers and stuffed them back in the envelope, hesitating for one moment before she took a piece of notepaper and scribbled a few words on it and shoved it in with her divorce papers.

Knowing she was doing the right thing gave her the strength to turn and hand over the package to Adam.

"Can you give these to Justin for me?"

The tic in his jaw was the only sign that Adam wanted to argue with her. In the end he nodded, taking the papers from her with a grimace. "You matter to Justin. He loves you and he will remember you. He'll miss you. These papers won't change that."

She laughed, wiping the tears away as she reached for her bag and the keys to her bike. He was right. The stuff in his hand was just paper and ink, words that did nothing to change the pain settled in her chest. "Those papers aren't meant to help Justin get over me, they're what I need to get over him."

Seventeen

Sarina had just vanished.

Justin stood in the doorway to the room she'd made her own the last few weeks. He stared at the bed where they'd made love and he'd given his heart away without even realizing it. They'd been happy together.

And for the first time in his life he'd been good enough just as he was.

And now she was gone with her motorcycle and her dog and all the ways she'd made his life complete.

All because he was a coward.

He'd been stuck at the party until the early-morning hours, making sure Aerospace Link wasn't going to jump ship and bail. Adam had disappeared and it had been impossible for Justin to leave.

The investors hadn't been happy with the news of his quickie Vegas marriage, most of them giving him disapproving looks that rivaled ones he'd received from his father over the years. At first he'd downplayed the whole night in Vegas, omitting the parts about the alcohol that fueled their matrimonial bravado and emphasizing the instant connection with Sarina.

He'd found himself telling them about how amazing his wife was. They'd heard about her separation from Adam and Roan and while he didn't get into the details of her life, he'd relayed how she'd grown up in foster care and then joined the army and served her country with bravery and loyalty.

And then he'd found himself telling them about her work with the kids at the center, how she loved his Nana Orla, and even how she'd found a dog behind a dumpster in some tiny little town in Nevada and now spoiled it rotten with love and cuddles. And he'd told them about how she loved Linda Ronstadt and that the best moment in his life was seeing her smile on the beach in Malibu while an old beat-up CD of *Heart Like a Wheel* played in a constant loop on the stereo system.

And that was when he'd known that he had just made the biggest mistake of his life.

Justin would never forget the shocked looks on

their faces when he'd stood up from where they were all seated and announced that he was going to find his wife and tell her that he loved her and beg her not to sign the divorce papers. He'd made it clear that if the deal was off, he understood, but he didn't care.

They'd blown his mind when they'd shoved him towards one of the property golf carts and told him to go get her. The deal was solid. Now was the time to save his marriage.

And so he'd raced home, not surprised when all of his calls to her had gone straight to voicemail. He'd pleaded with her to just wait for him, that he didn't want to finalize the divorce. He'd not told her that he loved her. Justin wanted the first time he said it to be in person, with her in his arms and agreeing to forever with him.

But he'd been too late.

Now, with the sun rising over the hills, Justin walked over to the large bay window and looked over the expanse of landscaped gardens and lawns, seeing Sarina everywhere. On the patio by the pool. Walking in the orchard with Nana Orla or playing with Wilma on the grass. If he focused he could see the tree house just on the edge of the horizon, the place she'd turned into magic. He reached up and rubbed the palm of his hand over his chest, trying to massage out an ache that he knew had nothing to do with the physical. It was marrow-deep. Painful. Permanent.

"Justin."

He turned quickly, almost falling off balance with surprise. Adam was standing in the doorway, his face taut with anger and eyes soaked in disappointment. Everything about his posture, ramrod straight and muscles tense, radiated how much effort it took for him to maintain his control. Adam had never raised a hand to him but Justin braced himself for the blow. He deserved it.

"Adam." Justin motioned around the empty room, everything about Sarina gone except the lingering trace of the citrus-sweet scent from her shampoo. She was on the run. Again. "She's just gone."

His voice cracked on the last word and he didn't even try to cover it up. He'd spent his life hiding how he was really feeling, protecting himself with a quick smile and the pretense that nothing touched him. This was killing him and he had nothing, no joke or defense or mask. His hand was exposed for all to see and he'd gone all in and lost.

Adam cocked his head to one side, his eyes narrowing into laser-focused slits as he examined Justin like he was a specimen at the zoo.

Heartbroken Homo sapiens. Genus Dumbass.

"Jesus, Justin."

He could see the anger leach out of Adam's body, replaced with sympathy and pity. He'd thought Adam being pissed at him was the worst but he'd been wrong—this was worse.

"Adam, if you have any idea where she's gone,

please tell me. I have to get her to talk to me. I have to explain and tell her I'm sorry." He approached his best friend, the man who was like a brother to him, raking his hands through his hair in frustration and rising panic. "I know you're pissed at me and I deserve it but you've got to help me find her." His voice wavered again, his emotions spilling over the dam after a lifetime of keeping them bottled up. "I don't know how you did this, man. When Tess walked away, how did you breathe?"

"Justin, I—" Adam broke off, his gaze drifting to the window and then back to his face. "Sarina asked me to bring these to you."

Adam held out a manila envelope to him. Justin's name was scrawled across the front in Sarina's sharp, dark handwriting and he knew immediately that he didn't want whatever was in that envelope. He took a step back and shook his head.

"Justin, take it. I saw her before she left town. I tried to get her to stay with us but she was determined to leave as soon as possible. She made me promise to give this to you."

"Adam, why didn't you keep her here? I know I fucked up and you want to kill me but you should have thought of some excuse to hold her up and called me."

"Yeah, right. Like I had any chance of keeping Sarina here when she was determined to go." Anger was back in his tone as Adam thrust the papers at him. "You did fuck up, Justin. I'm not going to force her to stay so that you can shit on her again. I wasn't thrilled when I heard about your marriage but I've watched you two together the last few weeks and it was good, man. You were good for her and she was good for you. You were amazing together." Adam's voice dropped lower, and he shook his head with obvious disappointment. "I love you like a brother, Justin, but I saw Sarina's face when you denied all of that last night and I don't know if I ever want to give you the chance to make her feel like that again."

"Adam, I'm so sorry." He had some apologizing to do and it needed to start with Adam. "Look, I made the wrong move tonight. I panicked when the reporter showed up and brought my biggest fear to life right in front of the Aerospace Link partners. Sarina and I hadn't talked about our next steps. We both kept putting it off because we didn't want to ruin how good it was, so I defaulted to a conversation we had weeks ago and ignored everything that had happened between us." He ran his hands through his hair, sitting down on the bed to get off legs suddenly too wobbly to hold him up. The adrenaline was wearing off and all that was left behind was bone-deep weariness. "I should have told the reporter 'no comment' and talked to Sarina but I didn't. All I could think about was the deal and the people who depended on us and I didn't want to be the reason we let them down. I couldn't be the fuckup again."

Adam settled beside him with a deep sigh, his voice scratchy and gruff with the fatigue of the last twenty-four hours. "Justin, you're not a fuckup. You're bold and energetic and you do things that nobody else can do because you're willing to take the risks necessary to make it happen." He nudged him with his elbow, pausing until Justin turned to look at him. "It's why we work so well together. I'm cautious but you push me and our company to be innovative and that has made all the difference in our success. You're not reckless, you're brave. If something gets fucked up then we fuck it up together just like we've done since college. I wouldn't do this with anyone but you. We're in this together. That's how it works."

Justin nodded, wondering how he'd lost sight of the way things were between them. He'd let the voices of his parents and all the crap they'd piled on him over the years drown out the fact that Adam believed in him and always had.

"Thanks, Adam. I came clean with the Aerospace Link people, told them that I didn't want to divorce Sarina. They were fine with it, practically drove me here themselves."

"Good. I knew you'd fix it," Adam said, his jaw tense with the frown that returned with the mention of the situation with Sarina. "Business is business. But the bigger issue is, you hurt my sister. Why should I trust you not to do it again?"

Justin deserved that. He struggled with the words

to make Adam believe that he was sorry, that he was the guy he could trust with Sarina's heart. There was only the truth. It was the only thing that had any chance to set him free.

"I love her, Adam," Justin said, his words loud in the empty room. "I *love* her. With everything I am."

Adam observed him, letting the revelation settle between them. A new truth between old friends. Finally, he sighed, reaching out to pull Justin into a hug. They stood that way for several long moments before Adam spoke.

"I'm sorry, man."

Justin pulled back, finally taking the envelope from him, turning it over and over in his hands. His gut told him that he knew what was inside. He glanced up at Adam, huffing out a heavy breath as he peeled back the sealed flap of the envelope and pulled the papers out.

Their divorce papers. Sarina's signature stood out, decisive and final in bold strokes of black ink.

Damn.

"She put a note in there, I think," Adam said, gesturing toward the envelope. "She wrote one. I saw her."

Justin riffled through the papers, heart sinking when he didn't find a note. He tipped the envelope over, shaking it. Something that felt like relief coursed through him when a half sheet of paper slid into his hand. He turned it over, eyes skimming over what she'd written.

Justin—I'm going back on the road to find my future. Thank you for the place to land even if it was only temporary. You're good enough. More than enough. Sarina.

"What did she say?" Adam asked, concern etched over his features. "It's good that she wrote a note, yeah?"

Justin turned it over in his mind. Was it a good thing that she wrote a note? All she had to do was sign the papers. The note had to mean something, didn't it?

"I think it has to be a good sign, Adam, but it doesn't matter. I'm going to find her anyway." Justin motioned toward the door. He was going now. He wasn't wasting any more time reading papers that he was never going to file. "I've got to go."

Justin headed toward the door, his mind going over every conversation he'd had with Sarina searching for a clue about where he could find her. He knew her and if he could just focus for a minute he'd figure this out. But time was flying by and with every minute she was on her bike and putting distance between the two of them.

Adam was right on his heels, pulling his phone out of his pocket. "Let me call Tess. She'll know how to search for Sarina. She found her once. She can do it again."

Justin entered the family room, looking for Nana Orla. He would say a quick goodbye and then hit the road. Only she wasn't alone.

"Mom. Dad. I didn't know you were here," he said, walking over to where his nana sat to give her a hug goodbye. "I can't stay. I've got to go and find Sarina."

"That's why we're here, Justin," his father said, tone firm with the conviction that whatever he was going to say was correct. "We need to talk about your marriage to Sarina."

"Dad, I know what you're going to say, so I can save you the time. She's not right for me and I need to just get divorced and marry someone like Heather." He held his hands out in a how-am-I-doing? gesture that he knew would piss off his parents. The only difference was that today he didn't care. Not anymore. "That's never going to happen. I love Sarina and I'm going to go find her, beg her to forgive me, and come back and build a life together."

"Justin, think about this. She's not the wife you need by your side." His mom looked beyond him to where Adam stood, her smile apologetic and expression sincere. "Adam, we mean no offense to your family. Sarina is a wonderful girl, I'm sure. She's just not what Justin needs. He needs someone who is more polished and familiar with the social circles you both have to navigate now. Justin needs a cool head, someone who will protect him from his worst impulses. I'm sure you agree."

Adam scoffed, shaking his head as he walked farther into the room. "No, Mrs. Ling, I don't agree. Sarina and Justin brought out the best in each other. I couldn't have asked for a better man for my sister and I think he's lucky to have her."

"We're not here to disparage your family, Adam. That's not the point," Allan Ling interjected in obvious frustration. His face was flushing red as he stood up from where he sat on the sofa. He focused his stare on Justin. "It is time for you to understand and accept your responsibility to this family, Justin. What you do reflects on all of us and it is time for you to stop putting yourself first and think of others. It is already all over town that you ended up in this drunken sham of a marriage. How am I supposed to do business with these people when they read your exploits in the tabloids? Why should your brothers and sisters have to hope that your behavior doesn't negatively impact their livelihoods? The circles we run in are small and memories are long. Your honor and reputation are all you have in the end, it's what keeps you on top."

Justin was done. The things he needed to say were long overdue. "Mom and Dad, I've spent my whole life worrying about reflecting poorly on the family and I'm done. I work hard and it's not good enough. I build a successful business with Adam and we land on the front page of *Forbes* and it's not good enough. I help kids who have nobody in their corner and it's not good enough." He held his hand up when his father moved to interrupt him. "No, I'm not finished. I understand that you want the best for me and I know that you sincerely think you know what that is, but you don't. You think the best thing for me is playing it safe, traditional, the road trampled by the million others on the same path, but you're wrong. I'm never going to do it the way everyone else does. I'm different. I've had to find my own path and I'm so damn proud of what I've accomplished, what Adam and I are doing." He took a deep breath, getting to the heart of it, and he could almost hear Sarina whispering in his ear. "I work every day to leave this world a little better than I've found it. I'm a good man, friend, boss, and God willing, I'll be a good husband. I don't know what the future holds for me because I'm open to any possibility but I do know that I can't—won't—do it without Sarina. I love her. She looks at me and I know I'm good enough because I have her love. If that's not good enough for you, then you need to live with the fact that you won't be a part of our lives."

"Justin," his mother sniffled, her cheeks wet with her tears and her voice choked with emotion. "We just don't want you to make a mistake."

He walked over and sat down next to her on the couch, pulling her against him in a hug. "Dad's parents thought you were a mistake and look at how wrong they were. You two came to the United States because you weren't accepted by his family but you loved each other too much to walk away. You proved them all wrong. I would think that you would understand."

"It wasn't always easy, son," his dad said, staring down at the woman he'd defied his family to love. "We want it to be easier for you, Justin."

"I don't need it to be easier. I just need it to be with her," he answered. "A hard day with Sarina is better than easy with anyone else. I think you both know that I'm right. It's what you lived every day right in front of me. I just want a chance to have what you have." He smiled at his parents, hoping that they were really listening to him. "I don't want to do it without you, but I will."

He let that sit in the air between them. He'd said his piece and his parents knew where he stood. He loved them but he also loved Sarina. If he had to choose, it wouldn't be an easy choice but it would be a clear one.

"Allan. Saoirse." Nana Orla spoke out from across the room and they turned to look at her. Her usually cheerful expression was gone, replaced with equal parts censure and compassion. She spoke slowly, her words clearly chosen with care and love. "I don't know if you know how proud I am of you both. I watched you struggle with loving each other and knowing that you'd have to give up so much to be together. You taught your children, you taught me, how important love is and that it's worth fighting for. You've raised a son who knows the value of love, the real kind of love that makes you want to be better. The kind that makes you stronger. I've watched Justin and Sarina together for weeks and they remind me of the two of you. If you don't see that, you're blind. If you don't give them your blessing, then you've been living a lie."

His parents looked at each other, several decades of marriage and love allowing them to communicate without words. He'd seen this a million times over his lifetime, finding it fascinating and terrifying at the same time. Whatever passed between them was settled with a nod from his father and another round of sniffles from his mother.

"Justin, do you have any idea where Sarina could be?" his father asked, his question settling it all between them.

He shook his head, memories of his wife ping-ponging around in his head as he searched for the answer. She had her bike and Wilma; she could be going anywhere. He picked up the note, reading it over again, letting the words sink in.

"She said she was going to find her future…"

And suddenly it was crystal clear.

"I know where she's going." Justin stood, scooping up the papers and calculating how much of a lead she had on him and how fast he could get there.

If he hurried he could intercept her and beg her to come home with him. It was worth a shot. Sarina was worth everything. "I need to hurry and I need a helicopter."

Adam grinned from across the room, pulling out his phone to make the call. "Luckily, we have one."

Eighteen

Justin Ling had ruined the Grand Canyon for her.

Sarina stood on the Skywalk, the glass bridge cantilevered seventy feet beyond the west rim, and glanced down at the view beneath her feet. Only air came between her and the valley of the canyon four thousand feet below. This place had been on her bucket list, one of the most anticipated stops on her road trip and she'd headed straight here after leaving California a couple of days ago, but she couldn't get beyond the tumult of thoughts banging around in her mind to register the beauty. A perfect combination of man-made genius and creator-formed nature, this Skywalk should have taken her breath away.

But she couldn't breathe around the pain ripping through her chest.

Dramatic? Yes.

Inaccurate? Damn, she wished.

The sound of a helicopter approaching from behind the visitor center caused the crowd to turn from the natural beauty to gape at the sleek black vehicle coming closer and closer and then lowering itself down to the ground. From where she stood, it looked like the bird had landed in the parking lot. Unmarked by any National Park Service logo, it had to be a private ride bringing someone here to the Grand Canyon for a VIP tour of the area.

Sarina couldn't help but remember the incredible weekend in Malibu with Justin. He'd orchestrated every move to make sure that she'd had the type of weekend only featured in celebrity magazines. The luxuries had been sweet but the way he'd looked at her, touched her, made love to her—those were the things she would never forget.

But she had to forget them. She had to put them behind her and move forward toward a life she could build for herself. For a minute she'd imagined that maybe she'd found a place where she could stop running, stop searching and put down roots. It had been a mistake.

That much Justin had gotten right.

A family walked past her, the young boy noticing Wilma with an excited tug at his mom's hand and a pointing finger. Wilma wagged her tail in excitement, standing on her hind legs and pawing at the air in the direction of her new friend.

"You can pet her if you want. She's friendly with kids," Sarina offered, watching closely as Wilma worked her magic and claimed another willing admirer.

Not for the first time did she wish she knew how Wilma still had this boundless joy for life and trust in people, even after she'd been abandoned and disappointed by an owner who should have done better by her. Once she would have scoffed at such optimism, counted it as the ultimate in stupidity to keep leaving yourself open for more heartbreak. But now Sarina knew that it wasn't foolishness—it was courage.

And even though she'd faced moments that teetered on the edge of life and death, risking heartbreak was scarier.

The little boy leaned over and hugged Wilma, pressing a loud, smacking kiss on her head before being led away by his mom. Wilma wagged her entire body at the kid, tugging at the leash to follow her new friend.

"Good girl." Sarina gave Wilma a scratch behind the ear, making a mental note to give her an extra treat when they got back to the bike. She glanced at her watch and realized that it was time to leave and get back on the road. If she was going to make Kingman, Arizona, before sundown she needed to go. She'd hang out there a couple of days and then she'd figure out where to head next. Anywhere was fair game. As long as she kept moving.

She needed to put miles between her and Justin. At some point she would stop feeling the pull to return to him and the tree house and Nana Orla.

She didn't belong there. No matter how much she wanted it to be the place where she belonged. She'd learned a long time ago that wishing didn't make anything true.

Sarina stood and turned to head back to the visitor center, squinting into the bright Arizona sun as she scanned the growing crowds of tourists. It was time to get back to the bike, grab some water for her and Willa, and hit Route 66.

"Sarina?"

The sound of her name stopped her in her tracks. Wilma tugged on the leash, whining in confusion at the sudden halt in forward momentum.

"Sarina."

She scanned the crowd, finally seeing the face that belonged to the voice when a family of four with "Brecken Family Reunion" T-shirts parted like the Red Sea and Sarina glimpsed the man who'd somehow become her promised land.

"Justin?"

Wilma whined louder and tugged even harder on the leash, the whines erupting into low growls as she fully recognized the man standing a short distance away. Sarina let Wilma pull her closer to Justin and unlocked the retractable leash so the dog could cover the last bit of distance between them. Justin loosened his white-knuckle grip on the Skywalk railing but didn't let go as he leaned over and patted Wilma on her head.

"Hey, girl, did you miss me?" Justin scratched behind her ears, huffing out a chuckle as she growled at him but leaned into the touch at the same time. "Well, that's progress, I guess." He pulled back his hand when Wilma bared her teeth and retreated to hide behind Sarina. "Or maybe not."

Justin straightened and moved closer to Sarina, his right hand wrapped around the railing as he shuffled closer to her one inch at a time. He was pale under the tan of his skin, every part of his body stiff with the fear she knew was coursing through him. For a guy who had a fear of heights, this had to be his worst nightmare on steroids.

"You had to pick a glass bridge four thousand feet over the fucking Grand Canyon, didn't you?" Justin complained, shooting an apologetic look at an elderly couple standing nearby. "Sorry, I don't like heights."

"No apology needed, son," the older man said, his expression entirely sympathetic. He glanced down at the silver-haired lady standing next to him, snaking an arm around her waist, then looked back at Justin and winked. "We do what we have to do for the women we love."

"Yeah, we do." Justin sneaked a glance at the glass floor under his feet and shuddered. Taking a deep breath, he turned and faced Sarina, moving to close the gap between them even more. He stopped when he was within arm's length of her. "I'm here to do what I need to do for the woman I love."

"Justin." She shook her head, refusing to let the hesitant bubble of elation in her belly cut loose. She'd been here before and nothing like this had ever worked for her. Sarina had opened herself up and hoped to be loved but it never worked out for her. She'd been that kid who'd allowed herself to hope that the next place she was sent would be the place where she was loved. But too many rejections in too many foster homes and the failure of her adoption had taught her that this wasn't for her. Not everyone got their happiness and that would have to be okay. So she couldn't let Justin's arrival raise her hopes again. She couldn't fall for it now. "What are you doing here? Didn't Adam give you the papers?"

Justin nodded, reaching into his back pocket and pulling out the mangled and folded envelope. He waved it in her face, his grin breaking through his panic over being on the Skywalk. "Got them."

"So what are you doing here? File them. Be done with it." Sarina shook her head, getting a little pissed off that they were even having this conversation. What had they been doing all these weeks if he was just going to walk around with the damn divorce papers in his pocket? "Justin, I don't know what's going on."

"I'm here to do this," he said, extracting the papers from the envelope and ripping them in half, and then in half again. He waved them at her and smiled. "I don't want a divorce."

Sarina shook her head, letting her anger break the surface and coat her words with the hurt and betrayal she'd carried with her since walking away from Justin at the winery.

"Well, I remember you saying something very different at the party. In fact, I think I remember you calling us *'a mistake.'*" She leveled a gaze at him intended to make sure that he would think twice about coming any closer. Tugging on Wilma's leash, she turned away from him and moved to exit the Skywalk. "This is your mistake walking away. Don't follow me. Don't contact me. Find a way to file those papers. Let me know when I'm cut loose from your ass. Have a nice life."

"Sarina, wait."

She kept walking. There was nothing Justin had to say to her that she wanted to hear.

"Sarina," Justin shouted, causing people to stop and turn to see the real-life drama playing out before them. Forget the Kardashians. The Redhawks and Lings were giving everybody a free show. "Sarina Redhawk, I want you to marry me."

Justin's voice carried, amplified by the slight echo created by the canyon. If anyone hadn't noticed their little scene yet, they were all riveted now. Conversations around them had dwindled down to murmured directions to be quiet and shushing sounds.

She didn't want to marry him but she wanted to strangle him. Was that an option?

Sarina turned to face down her husband, who now stood only two feet away from her.

"What the hell are you talking about, Justin? Thanks to you ripping up the divorce papers, *we are still married.*"

"I know. I know," Justin said in a calming voice, his hand extended in a gesture calculated to soothe but producing the opposite result. She was so tired of the games and drama.

"No, you don't know anything," she said through gritted teeth. "We made a mistake and now we can fix it. You don't want me, you just don't like losing. You don't like the fact that your family was right about us. Let it go, Justin. Let me go." She swallowed hard, stifling the emotions that pressed against her chest bone and shot pain up and down her body. "I need to go. I stayed too long."

"No. Sarina. You need to stay. With me." Justin reduced the distance between them a little more; now he was close enough for her to see the deep brown of his eyes, smell the smoky citrus of his cologne. "I told my family everything. I told them that I don't want a divorce and that marrying you was the best thing I'd ever done in my life. I told them that I love you and that you are my life. They are warming up to the idea and they'll get there eventually. Or not." He shrugged. "But you have to know, Sarina, I would have walked away from all of them and straight to you if they had refused to accept us. I choose you. Every time."

"What about Aerospace Link and the tabloid story?"

"I told the Aerospace Link people everything. They are completely on board and they won't care about the story because they know the truth. But even if they didn't, it wouldn't matter. I choose you, Sarina. Every. Single. Time."

Oh damn. He was close enough for her to reach out to him. If she did that he'd pull her into his arms and kiss her and make her feel like she was finally in a place where she belonged. A place where she was wanted. A place where she was the chosen one.

If she kept listening, he'd convince her to stay.

But she couldn't stay. Staying meant giving other people the option to tell her she didn't belong or to move on without her. She needed to go. Now.

So why couldn't she move?

Justin took her hesitation as all the permission he needed to continue. "Sarina, baby, marry me. Again. For real this time. Marry me with our eyes wide open. Marry me knowing all of my faults. Marry me in spite of my fear of heights, my meddling grandmother and my love of poker." Justin took two steps forward, lifting his hand to cover his heart. "Marry me because you make me feel like I'm good enough for the first time in my life. Marry me because you make me want to be a better person. Marry me and let me love you. Marry me and be my family and I swear I will always be yours."

Sarina closed her eyes, trying to erase the echo of his words in her brain and the bubbling joy running though her veins. She just needed to go. She needed to grab Wilma and get on her bike and keep moving until she was free again.

"Justin," she said, opening her eyes and looking at him head-on. She cringed at the wobble in her voice, clearing her throat quickly in an attempt to cover up just how hard this was for her. She loved him. She just couldn't stay. "I have to go. You know that."

"You want to keep running, Sarina?" Justin asked, his eyes searching her face.

Okay. Truth time. "I don't know how to stop, Justin. If I stop…"

She searched for the words to explain the panic and fear that washed over her. Justin closed the distance between them completely, raising his hands to cup her face. His eyes were focused on hers and then he smiled. That ridiculously wolfish grin that lit up his whole face and made her feel like she was the center of his world. That grin promised excitement and joy and laughter and acceptance.

Justin saw her. Fears and all. Prickly defense mechanisms and all. Scars and all.

"Sarina, baby, I'm not asking you to stop running. I'm just asking that you run to me." He leaned in and brushed a kiss across her mouth. "I love you, Sarina. Run to me. I promise you I'll always be here."

Sarina reached for him, her arms wrapping around his waist as she leaned up into his kiss. Justin hesitated for the briefest moment and then he slanted his mouth over hers, deepening the kiss with a groan. His hands slid from her face into her hair and the tug to give him better access was possessive and hot. Justin tasted like sin and safety, danger and homecoming.

He was her home. She'd found it in his arms and she'd never let him go.

Justin broke off the kiss and smiled at her as he released her. She protested the separation but her frustration turned to confusion as he dug around in his pocket, withdrew a small box and then dropped to one knee at her feet. Around them the crowd stirred into a wave of murmurs and gasps of surprise, and more than one cell phone was lifted and pointed in their direction. Sarina didn't care; she was laser-focused on Justin.

And he was focused on her.

"We didn't get to do this the traditional way the first time. I won't say that we did it wrong because it brought us together. So it was perfect. But I want to leave no doubt in anyone's mind that you are the one that I choose and the one I love." Justin opened the box and removed the ring, a square-cut sapphire surrounded by diamonds, reached out and took her hand and placed it on her finger. It was heavy but in all the best ways possible. "Sarina Redhawk, will you marry me?"

She was scared, terrified. But for the first time in her life she was more afraid of letting someone go without a fight. One word was all that was needed to take the leap and have a shot at the dreams she'd given up on a long time ago. This man was worth the risk. His love was worth the risk.

"Yes."

"Thank you." Justin rose to his feet and pulled her back in his arms, the kiss passionate and filled with laughter. He nodded at the crowd surrounding them, waving to those who held their phones up to film the proposal. Wilma barked and jumped around at their feet, wagging her tail in excitement. "I love you, Sarina Redhawk."

"It's Sarina Redhawk *Ling*," she answered, pressing a kiss to his lips. "I love you, too."

"Let's go home," Justin said, holding her hand as they navigated the crowd on the Skywalk. It was slow going, with everyone congratulating them and bending over to pet Wilma. "Fair warning. Nana Orla wants a wedding. She said that we couldn't come home if we didn't agree to have another wedding."

Sarina laughed, looking forward to a life with Justin. It would never be boring. "I can do a wedding. But not in Vegas. This time we do it right."

Epilogue

One month later

He'd marry her a million times over. Anywhere she wanted.

Sarina had looked beyond stunning when she'd walked down the aisle toward him just a few hours earlier. Wearing a white jumpsuit with full legs, a halter-style top with a plunging neckline, and a transparent, filmy train attached to the waist, she was the most beautiful woman he'd ever seen. He couldn't say that she was breathtaking because his every inhale and exhale, every heartbeat—they were for Sarina. Hell, the reason he got up every morning and hurried home each night was because of her. His wife.

Nana Orla had taken over the planning of the wedding, running everyone and everything in her orbit with a precision that rivaled the military. Now Adam wanted to hire her to head up their project management division at Redhawk/Ling. Justin was all for it if it would stop her from making a plea for another great-grandchild at every opportunity. He wanted a family with Sarina, wanted to build with her a life where their children knew they were loved and were always enough. But they had time. A lifetime together to make those dreams come true.

And today they were surrounded by two hundred of their friends and family, on the grounds of his family home.

"Nana Orla sure knows how to throw a party. This is amazing," Adam said, easing up beside him and handing him a beer. It was pretty epic and the hottest invitation of the year. Justin's only requirement was that the wedding not be held in a stuffy hotel, so their two hundred guests were gathered under several tents, with the entire lawn and pool area covered in white roses and lilies. The best catering in Silicon Valley and a live band at the reception ensured that everybody on the guest list was having a good time. Socialites and business colleagues mixed and mingled with a few of the kids from the Rise Up Center and some of Sarina's army buddies. Even Wilma was dressed to the doggy nines in a Chihuahua-sized tux jacket and rhinestone collar.

Roan eased up next to the two of them, saluting

them both with his drink. "I need to hire Nana Orla to handle my next gallery show. She's incredible."

"We couldn't have done this without her. And I was determined to make it official again with your sister as soon as I could." Justin turned and tapped his beer bottle against the one held by both his best friend and brother-in-law. They were family now. For real. "Thanks for pulling double duty today, brother."

"You bet," Adam laughed, wearing the light gray linen suit Justin had chosen for the wedding. "How many times has the best man also given away the bride?"

"It meant a lot to Sarina that you two were here to walk her down the aisle," Justin shared, knowing that it was a significant step for the Redhawk family to take together. Everything wasn't settled between them but they were all trying to replace the hard memories and the loss with new ones of love, and fun, and being together. Justin threw an arm around Adam's shoulders. "The next big event will be when your son makes an appearance. I can't believe you're going to be a daddy."

"I know, man. But I'm ready." Adam flashed the smile of a man who was happy and content as he looked over at where the bride stood with Tess. She was radiant in a gray silk dress, cut to highlight her pregnant belly. Sarina had been anxious to have Tess stand up with her at the wedding, given that there were just a few weeks left before her due date. All in all, it had been a family affair. "Are you two ready to be godfathers?"

Justin snorted out a laugh and shook his head, humbled by the request. "I hope you know that Sarina is the adult in this equation. I'm on tap to take him to get his first tattoo and pick up girls."

"Or boys," Roan added, winking at the two of them. "Why should he have to choose?"

"Truer words have never been spoken," Justin agreed, and Adam nodded his head in assent.

"I have to go to Washington, DC, next week but I'll be back in time to meet the newest Redhawk," Roan said, his smile definitely the one worn by the cat that ate the canary. "I've been summoned to the White House by President Irons to paint the official portrait of his daughter."

"Whoa. That's huge, little brother," Adam crowed, drawing the attention of several nearby guests. "How did you score that job?"

"How did you ever get cleared by the Secret Service?" Justin asked, acknowledging the raised middle finger of his brother-in-law with the salute of his beer bottle.

"President Irons is the first Native American president and he's determined to represent," Roan explained, flashing a shit-eating grin that made them all laugh. "*And* he picked the best of the bunch."

"And that's you?" Justin teased, unable to resist.

"Yeah, that's me," Roan answered, giving them both a big wink.

"Well done, Roan." Justin placed his beer bottle

on a nearby table and patted both of the men on the back. "Gentlemen, I'm going to dance with my wife."

He waved off their teasing farewells, making a short detour to the band and putting in a request before sauntering over to where Sarina chatted with Nana Orla and Tess. He eased up behind her and looped his right arm around her waist, placing a kiss on the soft skin of her shoulder. She leaned back into him, her fingers linking with his as they molded their bodies together. It was like he could only take a full breath when he was with her, like he only stood as a complete man when she was by his side. How had he thought he was living all those years before Sarina?

"Nana Orla, can I steal my wife for a dance?" he asked, smiling down at the woman who'd given a home to Sarina when she needed it the most. If he hadn't already loved his grandmother beyond reason, that would have sealed the deal.

Orla nodded, smiling at both of them as she reached up and placed a hand on his cheek. "Of course, my love. Go and dance with your best girl."

He shook his head. "Sarina and I agreed—she's the love of my life but *you'll* always be my best girl."

"Flatterer."

"It's not flattery if it's true." He pressed a kiss to her cheek and reached a hand out to his wife, still in awe that she was really his. "Sarina, dance with me?"

She smiled, an expression that lit up her entire face and made her dark eyes shine like onyx. Her raven-black hair was pulled back in a sleek ponytail, diamond earrings sparkling in her ears. A gift from his parents, they were a peace offering. It wasn't a perfect fix but it was a start.

"Forever," she murmured, stepping into his arms as the band started the slow-dance version of "Just One Look." The recognition of the song fueled joy on her face. They'd collaborated on a playlist but he'd secretly added all of her favorite Linda Ronstadt songs as a surprise. "Thank you for this."

"I wanted your mom—both of your parents— to be here with you today." Justin leaned in to press a kiss to the end of her nose, pretending not to see the sheen of tears in her eyes. "I know you wish they could be here."

"They're here, Justin," Sarina said, conviction in her voice. "I've felt them with me all day. How could they not be here when I'm so happy?"

"I promise you that I will spend the rest of my life making sure you're this happy every day," Justin said, soaking in her smile. "I love you, Sarina."

"I love you too, Justin." Sarina kissed him, long and sweet, the smile on her mouth a promise of forever. "Thank you for loving me, for being my family."

* * * * *

*If you loved Justin and Sarina's story
you won't want to miss Roan's!*

*Coming soon
from USA TODAY bestselling author
Robin Covington
and Harlequin Desire!*

* *

WE HOPE YOU ENJOYED
THIS BOOK FROM

⊕ HARLEQUIN

DESIRE

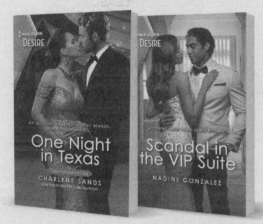

Luxury, scandal, desire—welcome to
the lives of the American elite.

Be transported to the worlds of oil barons, family dynasties, moguls and celebrities. Get ready for juicy plot twists, delicious sensuality and intriguing scandal.

6 NEW BOOKS AVAILABLE EVERY MONTH!

SPECIAL EXCERPT FROM

ⒽHARLEQUIN
DESIRE

*When a scandal jeopardizes playboy CEO Drew Maddox's
career, he proposes a fake engagement to his brilliant
and philanthropic friend Jenna Sommers to revitalize his
reputation and fund her efforts. But as passion takes over,
can this bad boy reform his ways for her?*

Read on for a sneak peek at
His Perfect Fake Engagement
by New York Times *bestselling author Shannon McKenna!*

Drew pulled her toward the big Mercedes SUV idling at the curb.
"Here's your ride," he said. "We still on for tonight? I wouldn't
blame you if you changed your mind. The paparazzi are a huge pain
in the ass. Like a weather condition. Or a zombie horde."

"I'm still game," she said. "Let `em do their worst."

That got her a smile that touched off fireworks at every level of
her consciousness.

For God's sake. Get a grip, girl.

"I'll pick you up for dinner at eight fifteen," he said. "Our
reservation at Peccati di Gola is at eight forty-five."

"I'll be ready," she promised.

"Can I put my number into your phone, so you can text me your
address?"

"Of course." She handed him her phone and waited as he tapped
the number into it. He hit Call and waited for the ring.

"There," she said, taking her phone back. "You've got me now."

"Lucky me," he murmured. He glanced back at the photographers,
still blocked by three security men at the door, still snapping photos.
"You're no delicate flower, are you?"

"By no means," she assured him.

"I like that," he said. He'd already opened the car door for her,
but as she was about to get inside, he pulled her swiftly back up
again and covered her mouth with his.

His kiss was hotter than the last one. Deliberate, demanding. He pressed her closer, tasting her lips.

Oh. Wow. He tasted amazing. Like fire, like wind. Like sunlight on the ocean. She dug her fingers into the massive bulk of his shoulders, or tried to. He was so thick and solid. Her fingers slid helplessly over the fabric of his jacket. They could get no grip.

His lips parted hers. The tip of his tongue flicked against hers, coaxed her to open, to give herself up. To yield to him. His kiss promised infinite pleasure in return. It demanded surrender on a level so deep and primal, she responded instinctively.

She melted against him with a shudder of emotion that was absolutely unfaked.

Holy crap. Panic pierced her as she realized what was happening. He'd kissed her like he meant it, and she'd responded in the same way. As naturally as breathing.

She was so screwed.

Jenna pulled away, shaking. She felt like a mask had been pulled off. That he could see straight into the depths of her most private self.

And Drew helped her into the car and gave her a reassuring smile and a friendly wave as the car pulled away, like it was no big deal. As if he hadn't just tongue-kissed her passionately in front of a crowd of photographers and caused an inner earthquake.

Her lips were still glowing. They tingled from the contact.

She couldn't let her mind stray down this path. She was a means to an end.

It was Drew Maddox's nature to be seductive. He was probably that way with every woman he talked to. He probably couldn't help himself. Not even if he tried.

She had to keep that fact firmly in mind.

All. The. Time.

Don't miss what happens next in…
His Perfect Fake Engagement
by New York Times *bestselling author Shannon McKenna!*

Available March 2021 wherever
Harlequin Desire books and ebooks are sold.

Harlequin.com

HDEXP0221